Pricilla took a step back from the body. There was no doubt about it. Reggie Pierce was dead.

She squeezed her eyes shut. It was happening again. A mere seven months ago she'd seen Charles Woodruff's lifeless body slumped in a wingback chair beside one of the fireplaces at the lodge. Charles Woodruff's death had been enough to leave her on edge, and now a second dead body. . . Maybe if she concentrated hard enough she would be able to wake up and all of this would be nothing more than a bad dream. She counted to five then opened her eyes again.

Reggie still lay in the same spot.

Other mysteries by Lisa Harris

Recipe for Murder

Don't miss out on any of our great mysteries. Contact us at the following address for information on our newest releases and club information:

Heartsong Presents—MYSTERIES! Readers' Service
PO Box 721
Uhrichsville, OH 44683
Web site: www.heartsongmysteries.com

Or for faster action, call 1-740-922-7280.

Baker's Fatal Dozen

A Priscilla Crumb Mystery

Lisa Harris

HEARTSONG
PRESENTS
MYSTERIES

A big thanks to Susan, Lynette, Rhonda, and Darlene.
I'd be lost without your honest critiques. And to my
mom. Thanks for always being there for me.

ISBN 978-1-59789-712-9

Scripture taken from the HOLY BIBLE, NEW INTERNATIONAL
VERSION®. NIV®. Copyright © 1973, 1978, 1984 by International
Bible Society. Used by permission of Zondervan. All rights
reserved.

All of the characters and events in this book are fictitious. Any
resemblance to actual persons, living or dead, or to actual events
is purely coincidental.

Cover design: Kirk DouPonce, DogEared Design
Cover illustration: Jody Williams

*Our mission is to publish and distribute inspirational products
offering exceptional value and biblical encouragement to the masses.*

Printed in the U.S.A.

Pricilla Crumb snatched a pile of envelopes from the mailbox and shivered in the chilly May breeze. A letter from Max Summers rested on top. She sighed in frustration. She'd come to the conclusion that a long-distance relationship was no different than the *Titanic* on that fateful night it struck an iceberg. Both were poised for inevitable disaster. That, in her mind, described her relationship with Max Summers. Seven months ago they decided to try to move beyond their thirty-year friendship and give love a chance. After being married to her first husband for over four decades before he died, Pricilla had come to believe that life didn't give second chances when it came to true love. Max had changed all of that—for a while anyway.

Making her way up the front steps of her son's two-story hunting lodge, she shoved the stack of correspondence under her arm then ripped open the red envelope that had Max's return address on the front. Yanking out the birthday card, she eyed the picture of a cake and a plump baby staring back at her.

Pricilla sat down on one of the padded wicker rocking chairs on the porch and read the card. "To another sixty-five years of feeling young at heart."

While the sentiment was appreciated, turning sixty-five had never felt quite so. . .well, so old. She could tolerate the blood pressure pills and the occasional Metamucil. It was the glance in the mirror this morning that had reminded her that while she might still feel young at heart, her body had decided to grow old without her. Not that she wanted to return to the age of high heels and miniskirts. Not at all. But an occasional day without having to wear bifocals would be nice or, at the very least, being able to remember where she put them.

And it wasn't as if she didn't appreciate the card either, because she did. The same as she looked forward to her biweekly phone calls with Max. The problem was that their relationship had hit a slump of predictability. They'd both decided that at some point, if they wanted their relationship to continue, they'd have to figure out a way to shorten the miles between them. But that meant one, or both, of them would have to move. And neither of them, it seemed, was ready to make the transition.

Max, who wasn't fond of the cold Colorado winters, dreaded the idea of giving up the warmer climate of New Mexico. Pricilla's temporary job of cooking for her son's lodge had saved her from the mundane routine of retirement and was currently in a state of semi-permanence, something she was quite happy about. Cooking had been her passion since she won the first annual Rocky Mountain Amateur Chef Competition thirty-five years ago, before she'd moved to Seattle and started teaching at the Willow Hill Private Academy for Girls.

She flipped the card back open and read the last sentence again. *Try to stay out of trouble until I see you again! Love, Max.*

Pricilla chuckled, realizing exactly what he was implying, but he had no need to worry as she had no plans to get involved in another whodunit. Frankly, her experience in helping to solve Charles Woodruff's murder left her believing that crime solving really should be left to the authorities (with the exception of Detective Raymond Carter), and that her ability to solve the case was nothing more than a coincidence.

Penelope, her Persian cat, jumped up on her lap and yawned, as her son Nathan clambered up the porch steps in his work boots.

"Good morning, Nathan."

"Good morning, Mom." He plopped down beside her then rested his boots on another chair.

Even at seven in the morning, she knew he'd been up for hours, making sure things at the lodge were ready for another day. With three newly hired trail guides, Rendezvous Hunting Lodge and Resort offered everything from horseback riding to fishing to hiking, and had become one of the premiere places to vacation in the mountains of Colorado.

Nathan took in a deep breath then lay back against the padded headrest. "Don't tell me you're making cinnamon rolls for breakfast."

"Complete with cream cheese frosting." She knew he couldn't resist her breakfast specialty. "It was a request from one of your guests."

Pricilla glanced at her watch. They still needed another ten minutes to bake, but already the sweet scent of the baking rolls wafted out the front door, and her stomach rumbled.

"Maybe I need to put in a few more special requests." Nathan was six feet two and, since childhood, had never seemed to get his fill of food. "I don't remember the last time you made some of those gooey rolls for me."

"You'd better watch what you're saying." She handed him the mail, keeping Max's card for herself. "If I'm not spoiling you, Trisha is."

"I am a lucky man, then." Nathan glanced at the card she held. "A card from Max?"

"Yes."

"How is he?"

She tapped the envelope against the palm of her hand. "He's doing well. I'll tell him you asked next time he calls."

"Tell him he missed the birthday party I threw for you last night—"

"Nathan, that's not exactly fair."

Her son tended to be overly protective of her, something that amused her greatly, considering she remembered the exact complaint coming from his mouth as an independent teenager. Besides, Max had planned to fly up for her birthday until two old buddies invited him to go on a fishing trip to Lake Pleasant. She'd insisted he join them, and after hesitating, he promised to fly up to Rendezvous in a couple weeks to see her.

Nathan's frown made it clear how he felt. He never could keep his feelings to himself. "I just don't think that phone calls are good enough. I've never believed in long-distance relationships."

"People do it all the time."

He started flipping through the mail, his frown still in place. "Why don't the two of you make the move? Trisha was hesitant about moving to Colorado, but she loves living here now."

No matter where she and Max were in their relationship, Pricilla was certain she'd been right on track when she decided to put her matchmaking skills to the test between Nathan and Trisha, who also happened to be Max's only daughter. Sparks between them had ignited the moment they met, and she was convinced that Trisha was the perfect antidote to her son's once lonely heart. The girl was not only beautiful with her highlighted hair that accented her skin tone to perfection, she was also smart, efficient, and—

"Why doesn't Max make the move?"

Now Pricilla was the one to frown. "Moving when you're thirty is one thing. Once you get to be our age, moving from the couch to the bedroom can become an ordeal."

"And that's coming from the woman who's making my lodge a success with her gourmet three-course meals and to-die-for cinnamon rolls?" Nathan laughed. "What is it you're worried about this morning, Mom? Your birthday? You might have just turned sixty-five, but you're hardly ready for the geriatrics' ward."

"I never said I was. But every May twelfth I turn another year older. While it's not exactly something new for me, I do have to deal with the fact that my body's aging faster than my mind."

She patted the back of her hair, as if it were a case in point, and made a mental note to make an appointment at Iris's Beauty Salon for tomorrow afternoon. It was time for another perm, and maybe she'd do something different this time. She could have it colored black or maybe burgundy. . . .

It was time to get the focus of the conversation away from her and Max. "So when are you going to ask Trisha to marry you?"

"When the time is right." He leaned forward as if he were afraid Trisha would hear him despite the fact that she was a dozen miles away in her condo in the mountainous town of Rendezvous. "I bought the ring."

"That's a good first step." At least one person in their family was making progress in a relationship. "Now you have to ask her."

"I'm just waiting for the perfect moment."

Pricilla stopped rocking. Maybe that was the problem with her and Max. Maybe they were waiting for the perfect moment for everything to fall together. Something told her, though, that the perfect moment would never come unless they made it happen.

After her first husband, Marty, died, she'd eventually found the strength to be grateful that the good Lord had lent him to her for over forty years. Still, while she'd never admitted even to Max that she was lonely, it was hard not to wonder at times what it would be like to share her life with him on a day-to-day basis.

~

Three hours later Pricilla headed into the small town of Rendezvous. With breakfast over and Misty, who'd moved up from housekeeper to Pricilla's full-time kitchen assistant, finishing the cleanup, Pricilla had time to pick up a few things in town for tonight's dinner. She'd already prepared ten sack lunches for those going on a day hike with one of the guides, so no one should need her until dinnertime.

While she sometimes missed the bustle of Seattle and its conveniences, she'd grown up in the Colorado Mountains and loved being back. She'd also gotten to know the owner of the local grocery store, who now went out of his way to order for her whatever she needed. Her menu choices had never been ordinary. Her favorite pastime was experimenting with everything from hors d'oeuvres like stuffed eggs and salmon-filled tartlets (which had almost gotten her arrested once), to spectacular desserts like caramel custard with flaming peaches or her famed lemon crumb cake.

Today, though, she had only one stop to make. The Baker's Dozen carried the best pastries and fresh bread from here to Denver, and while she couldn't say she particularly liked the proprietor, Reggie Pierce, and his overbearing ways, his cream fillings, in particular, were divine. And buying his fresh baguettes and sourdough loaves certainly saved her time in the kitchen.

Pricilla parked the car in front of the shop and breathed in the fresh mountain air as she stepped out of her car. Normally, with spring officially here, Rendezvous' population, which hovered just under three thousand, would drop slightly until the snows came again, but today, despite the fact that ski season was over, the streets still bustled with a few remaining tourists.

The bell on the door jingled as she went inside the bakery and caught the aroma of fresh yeast bread. A large glass case displayed every pastry imaginable. The

Baker's Dozen had become quite popular with not only the town and its tourists, but across the nation through its new Internet and mail order service. While Pricilla might know nothing about computers or how to use the Internet, Reggie's wife, her good friend Annabelle, had told her that Reggie predicted that their online business would soon surpass local sales in the shop.

Pricilla stood at the counter, wondering why there was no one in the room to help her. Normally, Reggie enjoyed running the front room himself, but today the only noise was the whirl of the ceiling fans above her. She tapped her fingers on the glass case and studied today's selection. While she preferred making her own desserts, the Italian shortbread cookies looked scrumptious. If nothing else, she would order half a dozen for herself. Of course if she ordered a dozen, Reggie would throw in one more for free. . . .

Pricilla frowned, wishing the counter had a bell she could ring for faster service. While most of tonight's dinner was already in the final stages of preparation, that didn't mean she had time to dawdle in town.

"Reggie? Hello?"

She glanced back at the door and noted that the CLOSED sign that hung on the glass was facing her. The shop should be open. She slipped behind the counter and through a small back room until she was standing outside on a tiled patio.

"Reggie—?"

That's when she saw him.

Pricilla couldn't breathe. Her stomach clenched.

Reggie Pierce lay on the tiled patio with a large vase smashed to pieces around his head, his face colorless with no signs of movement. Reggie Pierce was—at least in Pricilla's mind—dead.

2

Pricilla took a step back from the body. There was no doubt about it. Reggie Pierce was dead.

She squeezed her eyes shut. It was happening again. A mere seven months ago she'd seen Charles Woodruff's lifeless body slumped in a wingback chair beside one of the fireplaces at the lodge. Charles Woodruff's death had been enough to leave her on edge, and now a second dead body. . . Maybe if she concentrated hard enough she would be able to wake up and all of this would be nothing more than a bad dream. She counted to five then opened her eyes again.

Reggie still lay in the same spot.

She struggled to take a deep breath and wondered where the nearest phone was. Sheriff Tucker would have to be informed immediately. Pricilla leaned down and picked up a jagged piece from the broken terra cotta pot before looking up at the overhead balcony that led from the Pierce residence. Could one of the pots have simply fallen off the edge of the balcony, or had this been a deliberate act of murder?

Heels clicked on the tile behind Pricilla, and she turned around to see who was there.

"Reggie?" Annabelle Pierce, Reggie's wife, stopped halfway across the patio, her hands covering her mouth.

O Lord, please give me the right words.

"I'm so sorry, Annabelle. I'm afraid Reggie is. . .

he's dead." Pricilla closed the distance between them, wishing there were a way to undo what had happened. But there wasn't, and right now all she knew to do was keep a line of prayer open and continue to ask God for wisdom.

Annabelle leaned over the lifeless body of her husband, her chest heaving with emotion. "What happened?"

Pricilla shook her head. "I don't know exactly, but it seems that a pot fell from the balcony. We need to call—"

"911." Annabelle fumbled, trying to open her crocheted handbag, then dropped it, scattering the contents across the stone flooring. She fell to her knees. "If we hurry, maybe they can do something—"

"It's too late." Pricilla bent over Annabelle's slender form and tried to steady the sobbing woman.

Instead of being comforted, Annabelle feverishly started grabbing tubes of lipstick, tissues, and an assortment of other items and began shoving them back into her purse.

Pricilla picked up the cell phone that had slidden behind a potted plant and punched in 911. Annabelle certainly wasn't in the right frame of mind to make the call. When the phone failed to ring, she checked the face of the phone.

The battery was dead.

"Where are all the employees?" Pricilla asked. While she needed a phone, the last thing they needed was a bunch of people stumbling onto the outdoor patio and making a mess of the scene in case Reggie's death had been a crime.

"In the staff room." Annabelle's breaths came in ragged spurts. "Reggie had called a meeting, but when he didn't show up. . ."

"You came to look for him?"

Annabelle nodded her head.

"Mrs. Pierce, I. . ."A young man who looked to be in his late twenties stopped short at the edge of the patio. "What in the world. . . ?"

Pricilla stepped forward. "Mr. . . ."

"Robinson. Darren Robinson." The man pushed his thick glasses up the bridge of his nose. "I'm one of Mr. Pierce's employees."

"Darren, I'm Pricilla Crumb. As you can see, Mr. Pierce has. . .well. . .been involved in an unfortunate accident."

"The sheriff?" Darren walked toward the body. "Has he been called?"

"The battery's dead," Pricilla said, holding up Annabelle's phone. "And please, don't touch anything. The authorities will need to investigate the scene."

"Of course." Darren slipped a cell phone out of his pocket and turned to face her. "I'll make the call."

Annabelle stood and grabbed Pricilla's forearm. "Ezri and Stewart just returned from the university. They can't see their father like this. . . ."

"I just left them in the staffroom," Darren said.

Pricilla nodded, knowing it was up to her to keep everyone calm until the authorities arrived. "Darren, would you please bring Ezri and Stewart into the front bakery where we will wait for the sheriff? You also might lock that side door and let the other employees know what has happened."

"Certainly," he said with the phone to his ear.

With the rest of the employees taken care of for now, Pricilla led Annabelle into the shop, where she obediently sat on one of the wooden benches that lined the front windows. Pricilla flipped the sign in the window to CLOSED then took a seat beside the distraught woman. Everywhere she looked there were pastries, fresh baguettes, and donuts. The once-pleasing aroma of sweets that filled the room now made her stomach churn.

Her mind raced with the implications of what had just transpired. "Who was supposed to be minding the store?"

"I don't know." Annabelle stared at the busy pattern of the tiled floor. "Monday staff meetings were common. Reggie normally assigned someone to stay out front while we met. I never heard anything. How could I have missed it?"

"So you didn't hear a crash?"

Annabelle shook her head. "I don't know what I'm going to do now. And Ezri and Stewart. I'd looked forward to your meeting them, but now. . ."

Pricilla reached out and squeezed Annabelle's hand, wishing she were better at finding words of comfort. Annabelle had become a regular visitor at the lodge, coming to have tea at least once a week with Pricilla. But despite their newfound friendship, there were just certain things that one could never prepare for, and this was certainly one of them.

Pricilla wished she had her notebook. While she

was no expert on the intricacies of solving a case, she had been successful in catching Charles Woodruff's murderer and in the process had learned a thing or two. There was no doubt that because of their friendship, Annabelle would tell her things that she would never mention to the sheriff

Ezri and Stewart entered from the front of the shop. Introductions were brief. As they sat on either side of their mother and waited silently for the sheriff, Pricilla tried to remember what Annabelle had told her about her children.

Stewart was twenty years old and, according to his mother, lazy. He looked so much like his father with his dark hair and eyes that Pricilla couldn't help but wonder if he took after his father in other ways as well—like a bad temper and an overt fondness for material things. But the outward similarities stopped with his physical features. Reggie, always dressed neat and proper, would never have worn cutoffs and an old sweatshirt like the ones Stewart sported today.

Pricilla turned to study Ezri. She favored her mother as far as looks went. Tall and slender with short, kinky blond hair and blue eyes, she'd just finished her junior year at Columbia University, studying marketing. While Pricilla certainly didn't want to put either of Reggie's children on the suspect list, she also knew from their mother that neither of them had a good relationship with their father. And, if she remembered correctly, Stewart was studying forensic science. Was it possible he knew enough about criminal behavior from classes and online research to be dangerous?

Pricilla shook her head. Just because she'd once found herself involved in trying to solve a murder didn't mean that was the case again this time. Annabelle's children were the victims here, not suspects.

Five minutes later, and much to Pricilla's displeasure, Detective Carter arrived with the coroner. Sheriff Tucker, it seemed, was working another case and was currently unavailable. Pricilla had hoped that the chief himself would be free to investigate instead of sending his nephew, who, from the look on his face, felt the same way about seeing her. The two of them had clashed during Mr. Woodruff's case, where the detective thought Pricilla had no business being involved. That might have been true, but it wasn't as if she'd chosen to have another murder take place practically at her feet.

The glass door to the bakery clicked shut behind the detective. "Ahh, Mrs. Crumb, we meet again."

"So it seems, Detective."

He turned to Annabelle and her children. "Mrs. Pierce, while I know this is a difficult situation for you, I will need to get a signed statement from each of you. If you would go upstairs to your apartment while I make an initial examination of the scene and the coroner begins his investigation, I'll join you shortly." The detective addressed Pricilla again. "I will need a statement from you as well, Mrs. Crumb. Why don't you show us the body, then perhaps you could serve some tea to help calm everyone's nerves. You are proficient in the kitchen, are you not?"

"An award-winning chef, actually," Pricilla

murmured under her breath as she led the detective and the coroner out back.

Detective Carter surveyed the scene, shining a flashlight across the smooth stones. "A light shone on the ground at various angles, even outside in broad daylight, creates new shadows that, in turn, could expose evidence."

"Really." Pricilla wasn't impressed.

Leave it to Detective Carter to show off his knowledge of crime scene procedure. She normally didn't carry such a strong dislike toward people, but there was something about the detective that never failed to rub her the wrong way.

He let the beam of light follow the outer path of the broken vase. "What surprises me the most is how we meet again in such unpleasant circumstances, Mrs. Crumb."

"It's certainly not by my choosing."

The bald detective flicked off the flashlight then pulled out a spiral notebook from his back pocket and flipped it open. "Before I start my investigation, I need to know if you're planning to take the credit for Reggie's demise or if I should look elsewhere."

"Excuse me?"

His deep-throated laugh grated on her nerves. "It was a joke, Mrs. Crumb. Relax. Though I must say, even to a seasoned investigator, the fact that you're here once again at the scene of a murder does leave one to wonder if it's simply a coincidence. . .or something else."

Pricilla frowned at the statement. Just because she'd once believed she'd poisoned someone with her salmon tartlets and had foolishly admitted doing so to the detective didn't mean he had to bring it up. "I'm here because I'm the one who found Reggie's body."

Carter folded his arms across his chest. "Now this is getting more and more interesting by the minute. Did you know that statistically that means you are the one most likely to have killed him?"

Pricilla couldn't believe the man's ridiculous accusation. "No, I didn't know that, but I'm not a statistic."

"True, but I must caution you about one thing before I begin my investigation. I have to insist that just because you facilitated one or two aspects of Mr. Woodruff's case doesn't mean I need your help again."

"And I have no plans of offering it."

Maybe she wasn't a seasoned detective, but to speak to her as if she'd hindered his previous investigation instead of helped it wasn't right. If her memory served her correctly, which she knew it did, she was the reason Charles Woodruff's real murderer was behind bars.

"Detective, I need you to come take a look at something." The coroner knelt beside the body, his gaze focused on the deceased man.

"Why don't you go on up and wait with Mrs. Pierce," Carter said. "I won't be long."

Thankful to get away, Pricilla took the winding staircase that led from the back of the store up to Annabelle's spacious home. The upstairs apartment had changed little from the last time Pricilla had been here. On one of her previous visits, Annabelle had given her a complete tour of the four-bedroom residence with its formal décor.

There was one thing that was notably different, Pricilla observed as she stepped into the living room and noted the familiar leather couches, oriental rugs, and polished brass fixtures. Reggie, who'd had a bit of an obsessive-compulsive disorder, had always insisted that everything stay in its proper place. This morning, though, there was a sense of disorganization to the room. It wasn't something that the detective would pick up on, since he'd more than likely never been here before. To Pricilla, on the other hand, the subtle differences were obvious.

A stack of mail lay scattered on the floor beside the antique desk, throw pillows were out of place, and the couch didn't line up along the lines of the wood flooring. Something had happened in this room.

Annabelle stood alone beside the sliding glass windows that led to the balcony. "I told Ezri and Stewart to wait in their rooms for now. I need your help, Pricilla. Everyone in town knows how you saved Claire from going to prison for life and helped to find Mr. Woodruff's real murderer and—"

"I can't get involved in another official investigation." Pricilla leaned against the back of the couch and gnawed on her lip. Not only did she have no business getting mixed up in another case, she'd never hear the end of it from the detective, her son, or Max.

"You don't understand. I'm afraid. . .I think I know what happened."

Pricilla's brow rose in question. "The police haven't even determined whether or not it was an accident—"

"It couldn't have been an accident. I'd never keep

pots on the edge of the balcony." Annabelle wrung her hands together. "I'm only going to tell you this because you're my friend and I trust you. I'm afraid the police are going to find out that Stewart might have been involved. They had a horrible fight this morning, and then. . .and then Reggie told him he was cutting him out of his will."

3

Pricilla had tried to reach Max for the past three days, but a fishing trip with two of his buddies had cut him off from all forms of communication. So much for modern conveniences. She cradled the cordless phone against her ear and paced the lodge's recently renovated kitchen, waiting for Max to answer. He was due to return this morning, so with a bit of luck she'd be able to reach him before she had to leave for Reggie Pierce's funeral.

On the fourth ring, he finally picked up. "Hello?"

She clicked her black heels against the hardwood floor. "Max, it's Pricilla."

"Well, this is a nice surprise."

Pricilla couldn't help but smile at the sound of his voice. Her heart thudded, but this time it wasn't the menacing jolt of the *Titanic* bumping against an iceberg. No matter how difficult their long-distance relationship might be, Max still made her feel young and alive again. Maybe there was hope for them after all.

"How was your trip?" she asked.

"We just pulled in about twenty minutes ago. The weather was perfect and the fishing even better."

She heard the smile in his voice as she stopped in front of the counter to drum her nails against the hard surface, wishing she had something more pleasant to tell him in return. "I need to talk to you—"

"What's wrong?"

"It's not me. I'm fine, it's just that. . ."

Pricilla closed her eyes and wondered if this was really a good idea. The last thing she needed was for Max to worry about her—something she knew he would do once he found out what had happened to Reggie. Max had been far from happy with her involvement in the Woodruff case, but what else could she have done? Not only had her reputation as a chef been at stake, the future of her son's lodge had hung in the balance as well. If she hadn't stepped in, Charles Woodruff's death might very well still be labeled unsolved, like the case of the town librarian who'd been found dead eleven years ago on the bank of Lake Paytah, wearing a purple scuba diving suit.

"Do you remember Annabelle Pierce?" Pricilla began pacing the large kitchen again. "She and her husband own the bakery in town."

"I remember her. What was her husband's name. . . Reagan?"

"Reggie."

"Wasn't he a bit—"

"Obnoxious? Yes, he was."

Reggie's temper had put him at odds with most of the town at one time or another. He'd even been kicked out of a town hall meeting for arguing with the mayor over the newly proposed town dump. If it weren't for his melt-in-your-mouth baked goods, no doubt most of the town would have been in favor of ousting the man into the next county—or state for that matter.

Pricilla swallowed hard. It was time to get to the point. "I found Reggie dead outside his shop this morning."

Max's silence spoke volumes. She'd known he wouldn't be happy that she'd stumbled on another investigation, but it wasn't as if she'd intended to walk into the Baker's Dozen and find a dead body.

Pricilla filled a glass of water from the kitchen faucet and took a sip. "Annabelle asked me to help find out the truth behind her husband's death. She needs me to—"

Max groaned. "Annabelle needs you to be her friend. The police will solve the case." He paused. "I'm sorry. I don't mean to sound harsh, it's just that I worry about you."

"But don't you see? I'm in a position to help her. People will tell me things they'd never tell the police."

"That doesn't matter. Getting involved with the detective's job is only asking for trouble." Max was silent again for a moment. "Have you talked to Nathan and Trisha about this?"

"We had dinner together last night and the subject did come up."

"And. . ."

Pricilla hesitated. "They were cautious but understood my need to help Annabelle."

"Pricilla. . ."

She set her glass down with a thud. "All right, maybe *understood* isn't the right word, but they're not going to try and stop me."

"You know I can't stop you either, but I've tried to tell you this before. You're not Jessica Fletcher, and this isn't another episode of *Murder, She Wrote* where the story is wrapped up neatly at the end of the hour.

If Reggie's death was a crime, then there's a murderer involved, and in playing amateur sleuth, you could end up putting your life in jeopardy."

~

An hour later Pricilla stood beside Nathan and Trisha and tugged at the bottom of her bodice, wishing her one black dress wasn't so uncomfortable. Reggie Pierce's funeral had been attended by less than a dozen people, and there were now even fewer people at the graveside service. Of those who had managed to make their way down the gravel road to attend the short service, most looked as if they'd rather be anywhere but standing together on a patch of green grass, remembering Reggie's far-from-perfect life.

While it was not yet noon, the sun was warm enough to bring trickles of perspiration to Pricilla's brow and make her wish for a moment that she, like the majority of the town, had decided to stay home. Apparently, no matter how good Reggie Pierce's pastries and sour dough loaves tasted, the man simply wasn't liked by the people of Rendezvous.

Stewart stood beside his mother, dressed in black jeans and a T-shirt. The scowl on his face made Pricilla wonder just how deep the conflict between the father and son had run. Had Reggie's pledge to cut him out of his will been simply words spoken in the heat of the moment, or had he planned to follow through with his threat?

Ezri's face looked pale and void of emotion as she

held on to her mother's arm. What secrets had she held regarding her feelings toward her father?

And then there was Annabelle. While the spouse of a victim was often the first person to suspect in a murder investigation, Pricilla had dismissed that idea before ever allowing it to take root. Sixty-five years had given her more than purple trails of varicose veins in her legs and crow's-feet at her temples. It had given her an inherent insight into other people's character. And Annabelle was not a murderer.

With the monotone voice of the minister rambling on in the background, Pricilla replayed Max's last words to her on the telephone.

"If Reggie's death was a crime. . ."

Certainly being involved in Charles Woodruff's murder investigation had changed her perspective on life. She didn't want to automatically see a villain behind every bush, but even Annabelle was convinced that her husband's death hadn't been a simple accident. If that were the case, weren't the chances high that whoever had done the ruthless deed was right here among them?

Pricilla couldn't help but study the small number of guests surrounding the gravesite. She'd made no promises to Max. Surely observing the guests couldn't get her into trouble.

Several of the workers from the bakery stood toward the back of the group, including Darren. His help on the day of Reggie's demise had been welcomed, but she wondered why a seemingly intelligent man his age was stuck working in the back of a bakery. Several of the other workers had immigrated from Mexico. Were they grateful to Reggie for their weekly paychecks, or did they hold a different sentiment entirely?

Nathan nudged her with his elbow. "Mom, the service is over."

Yanked out of her thoughts, Pricilla looked around at the guests who were already beginning to leave and sighed. If she didn't stay focused, her sleuthing was going to get her into trouble. "I'd like to speak to Annabelle before we leave."

Nathan nodded. "Trisha and I will meet you at the car."

Pricilla waited until Annabelle had finished speaking to the minister. "Do you want to talk?"

Annabelle nodded then slid her hand into the crook of Pricilla's arm. They strolled back toward the funeral home in silence for the first several minutes. Aspen trees shimmered in the wind beside the perfectly manicured lawn, while the sweet scent of lilacs filled the air. On any other day, the scene would have been perfect. Today it did little to lift the heavy atmosphere that hovered around them.

It was Annabelle who broke the silence. "Detective Carter stopped by to see me this morning. Because of some other evidence that came up, the coroner opened a murder investigation into Reggie's death."

"Oh, my." While the words didn't truly come as a surprise, to hear her friend speak them aloud still chilled Pricilla's heart. "I'm so sorry. I know this has to be a frightening experience."

"Without a doubt, but it's more than that. His

death has made me face my own life. Everyone knows that our time here on earth is limited, but that's easy to ignore until something like this happens."

"When someone close to you dies, it's natural to examine your life." Pricilla skirted around a mud puddle left from the previous night's rain. "I remember feeling that way when Marty passed away."

But Pricilla hadn't had to deal with the added strain of a murder investigation.

Annabelle stopped and turned toward Pricilla. "You don't have to worry about where you're going when your time comes. Your faith is strong. I once gave my life to Christ, but lately. . .I just can't see God forgiving me for the way I've been living my life the past twenty-odd years."

"It's never too late."

"It's too late for Reggie." Annabelle started walking again along the path edged with blue and white columbine in full bloom. "When I first married him he was so different. I fell in love with him because he was ambitious, and yet he cared for those around him. I never expected success to consume him the way it did. His entire life started to revolve around making money. I'd hoped that moving here to a slower pace of life would help settle him, but nothing changed."

The silence hung between them until Annabelle spoke again. "I feel as if my entire body's being crushed. Like some python's squeezing the life out of me."

Normally, what to say had never been an issue for Pricilla, but at the moment, she had to struggle for the right words. "You don't have to do this on your own,

Annabelle. The Bible describes us all as weak vessels. Jars of clay. It's His power that allows us to be crushed from life's circumstances without being destroyed."

"I just don't know. It's so hard. I think Ezri's seeing someone, Stewart's not doing well in school, and neither will talk to me."

Pricilla squeezed her friend's hand. "Promise me you'll think about what I said?"

Annabelle nodded, slowing as they neared the entrance of the funeral home. "There was one other thing I needed to say to you. It was wrong of me to ask you to help. I was upset and not thinking straight. To even think that Stewart might have had something to do with Reggie's death. . . The thought is simply inconceivable. I shouldn't have said anything."

"Please don't worry about it. I understand."

Annabelle stopped outside the front door of the funeral home. "I suppose I should go back in and at least thank the staff."

"I'll plan to call you tomorrow and see how you're doing. And if you need anything. . ." Pricilla hugged her then headed toward the car where Nathan and Trisha waited for her.

Someone shouting at the back of the parking lot caught her attention. Two people stood beside a black sports car, arguing. Pricilla was about to ignore them when she realized one of them was Ezri.

Wondering why the young woman wasn't inside with her mother and afraid there might be a problem, Pricilla walked past the next row of cars to see what was going on.

The dark-haired man with Ezri banged his fist on the hood then jumped into the car. With a grind of tires against the gravel, he headed out of the parking lot.

Pricilla hurried across the uneven surface, trying not to choke on the car's exhaust fumes. "Ezri, are you all right?"

Ezri stood motionless for a moment, her eyes rimmed with tears. Finally, she brushed the back of her hand across her face and drew in a deep breath. "I'm fine. It was nothing, just. . ."

"Who was that man?"

"No one, just a friend." She reached out and gripped Pricilla's arm. "Please, Mrs. Crumb. You can't tell my mother about any of this. . .promise me, please."

"Will you at least tell me why you're so upset? All I want to do is help—"

"I'm sorry. I can't." Ezri turned and ran toward the funeral home, her heels crunching across the gravel.

Pricilla stared after her, wondering what exactly it was that she'd just seen, and why Ezri seemed so afraid.

4

Max tried to ignore the fact that the hired taxicab driver was hitting every bump in the dirt road leading up to the lodge and instead focused on the surrounding mountainous area. While he loved New Mexico, he had to admit that Colorado offered its own unique setting with its snowcapped mountains, pale aspen trees, and lazy rivers. Of course for him there was an even stronger draw.

Pricilla.

He'd never expected to fall in love with his good friend's wife, but it had been four years since Marty passed away, and he knew there was no turning back now. He closed his eyes for a moment and pictured her pervasive smile and boisterous laugh. Silver hair lying in perfect curls against the nape of her neck. Wide hazel eyes that took in far more than most realized. He let out a slow sigh. While the years had added wrinkles and age spots, he still found her beautiful and completely enchanting.

There was only one problem. Their relationship, which he'd boldly taken from a lifelong friendship to a budding romance over lunch at Tiffany's seven months ago, had begun to wither.

Max rested his hand against his suitcase and fiddled with the airline tag. The two hundred or so miles of topography between them had proven to be more of a hindrance than he'd ever imagined it could be.

Declarations of love rarely accounted for such practical matters, but moving forward had proved difficult for two retirees set in their ways. And he certainly wasn't getting any younger.

Frowning, he shifted his weight and tried to get comfortable in the worn leather seats. The truth was they both had their reasons. For starters, he hated the Colorado winters, and she wasn't fond of New Mexico's hot summers. Trivial, he supposed, in the light of love and companionship, but nevertheless the barriers did exist.

No matter what obstacles had come between them, though, Max felt his heart race as the lofty structure of the Rendezvous Hunting Lodge and Resort finally came into view, and along with it, a dynamic showing of God's masterpiece. Nestled into a grove of aspen trees, the popular tourist destination was framed with the stunning backdrop of the Colorado Rockies. For a hunter, the lodge was paradise.

The taxi pulled to a stop in front of the lodge. Max alighted from the four-door vehicle, wondering for the first time if he'd made a mistake by not informing Pricilla of his unscheduled arrival. Trisha, his daughter, had assured him that he was welcome to stay in her spare bedroom though it wasn't set up for guests. He, in turn, had assured her that all he needed was a bed and a shower. Thirty-five years in the military had taught him that he needed far less to get by on than most people could even begin to imagine.

With the driver paid and his bags unloaded on the wide, wooden porch, Max stepped onto the gray-tiled floor of the entryway. He rang the bell at the front desk before walking into the living room. From the heavy wooden ceiling beams to the rustic pine furniture to the unique cozy rugs, every room added to the ambiance of the mountain setting. The woody fragrance from the fireplace filled his senses. With Pricilla beside him, perhaps the long, cold winters wouldn't seem quite so chilly.

"Can I help you?"

Max spun around and smiled at the familiar voice. Today Pricilla wore a striking red and black pantsuit, and while her taste in clothes ran as bold as her personality, she always looked beautiful to him.

"Max?"

"Pricilla." How he'd let two hundred miles come between them, he had no idea. If he was half as smart as he'd like to think he was, he ought to pop the question right now and forget about all the obstacles that stood between them. "You haven't aged a day since I saw you last."

Pricilla stopped at the edge of the hardwood floor, and the corners of her lips formed a smile. "Either I'm dreaming, or I'm experiencing a sudden onset of Alzheimer's and forgot you were coming."

He'd always loved her sense of humor. "Neither. I wanted to surprise you."

He bridged the gap between them, ignoring the slight awkwardness of the moment, and ran his finger down her cheek before kissing her gently on the lips. "I missed you."

Pricilla pressed the back of her hair with the tips of

her fingers. "You know, you really should have called so I could have had a room ready for you, and—"

"You look beautiful." He set his bags down on the floor and took her hand. The delight in her expression was obvious. "I'm staying with Trisha because I didn't want to take advantage of your son. The rooms are for revenue, not for pining suitors."

"You always did know how to win a girl's heart, didn't you?" Her laugh reminded him of just how happy she made him when they were together. "Are you hungry?"

"Starved."

"Good." She laughed again. "Come into the kitchen. We just finished lunch, but I think there's enough left over for you."

He followed her down the short hall, where the smells of her tantalizing cooking filled the air. The cup of coffee and small package of peanuts the airline had offered hadn't been near enough. "What's on the menu?"

She glanced back at him before stepping into the large, open kitchen that had been remodeled last year. "Chicken with a Cajun cream sauce, angel hair pasta, and a new recipe I tried out for peach cobbler."

"Peach cobbler?" Max's stomach grumbled. "I knew I wouldn't be disappointed."

"So the truth comes out." She stopped and rested her hand against the granite counter. Her voice was stern, but there was a twinkle in her eye. "Did you really miss me or are you only here for my fine cuisine, Mr. Summers?"

He shook his head. "There's no competition there. I'd choose an evening with you and a loaf of stale bread over a five-star meal without you any day."

She beamed. "Good answer. Now wash your hands, and I'll dish you up some lunch."

She'd always amazed him. Cooking three meals a day for the guests and staff couldn't be an easy job, yet she always prepared something out of the ordinary. Pricilla cooked the way she approached life, with zeal and enthusiasm. Those traits were only two of many that had drawn him to her.

Misty Majors, Pricilla's full-time assistant, entered the kitchen with a stack of dirty dishes from the dining room. "Why, Mr. Summers. What a surprise. It's good to see you, sir."

Max hesitantly returned a smile to the young woman whom he'd once interviewed as a suspect in a murder case. Apparently age was irrelevant to her, because despite his experience in dealing with hundreds of such interviews, Misty's blatant interest in him had had him running out of the room like a coon with his tail on fire. "It's good to see you, Misty."

"It's been a long time."

His gaze returned to Pricilla. "Too long." It was true. Twice in seven months wasn't enough. He'd flown up to see her at Christmas time, and in return Pricilla had visited at the end of February, when they'd celebrated a belated Valentine's Day and for some unknown reason she'd managed to avoid the subject of a permanent commitment. Now he realized what a fool he'd been, taking the chance of losing her. He should have stated his feelings outright. If he planned on making things permanent between them, something was going to have to change.

Misty left the room as Max reached for a towel to dry his hands. "So how is Annabelle? I was sorry to hear about the loss of her husband."

"Annabelle?" Pricilla put her hands against her hips. This time she wasn't smiling. "I should have known."

"Known what?"

"That you had an ulterior motive."

"An ulterior. . .I'm sorry." Max paused. Pricilla had a way of knocking down his sense of diplomacy, but while there was nothing wrong with his concern, perhaps he had jumped into the subject too soon. "I'm just extremely curious about the fact that barely seven months after Charles Woodruff's death, you manage to stumble over another dead body."

"It's purely coincidence."

"Don't get me wrong, you're not on my suspect list." He shot her a smile. "I know you better than to think you did it. But there's a murderer on the loose, and with one solved case under your belt and dreams of being Jessica Fletcher in the back of your mind—"

"That's not true."

"Isn't it?" He didn't want to widen the point of contention between them, but he couldn't help but worry about her and her seemingly fearless attempts at playing the role of amateur detective. "I know that once you have something set in your mind it's nearly impossible to change it. I just want you to promise to let Carter handle this one."

"Like he handled the last one?" Her eyes widened. "The man's incompetent and you talk about my being the amateur—"

"I'm sorry." Max held up his hand. It was time to switch gears. "Let's not fight. I have a present for you."

"Bribery?" Gifts always brought a smile to Pricilla's face and today was no exception. "I have to admit I like the way your mind works."

"Let me eat, and then I'll show you."

After Max finished his second helping of her peach cobbler, Pricilla watched as he pulled a large, rectangular bag from his carry-on and set it on the dining room table. Her change in attitude had nothing to do with the gift. She'd never been able to resist Max's charm.

Her eyes narrowed as he unzipped the case. "What is it?"

"A laptop." He set it on the table, obviously proud.

She leaned in closer and squinted at the shiny silver machine. "A computer?"

Max nodded. "Sit down beside me."

"I don't need a computer."

"You just don't know you need it. We can communicate and send e-mails to each other. Once you get the hang of it, you'll love it."

Reluctantly, she took the chair beside him. Even though she'd thought once or twice how a computer could have helped her to solve Charles Woodruff's murder sooner, she still didn't see how such an apparatus could ever be of real benefit. She'd said it before, and nothing had changed. Computers simply ended up making people work harder rather than taking away some of the burden of labor. They were too complicated, too time consuming, and too antisocial. And besides, who wanted to be stuck in front of a screen all day?

She watched as Max pushed a button and the machine whirled to life. She supposed that she should at least try to seem interested. After all, he did travel all the way from New Mexico to see her. Something told her, though, that as innocent as Max appeared, he had a hidden agenda behind the surprise visit and the computer that tied back to the death of Charles Woodruff.

And now Reggie Pierce.

She tried to feign interest. "So you and I can send e-mails to each other?"

"E-mails, pictures, and that's just the beginning of what you can do. . . ."

Pricilla stared at the photo of a purple iris that filled the screen as she tuned out Max's voice. There was nothing wrong with her way of sending a letter. Flowery stationery, her favorite ink pen, and an hour in the garden were all she needed. She even loved the trip to the post office where she could choose what kind of stamp she wanted while catching up on all the latest news in town. No computer could do all of that for her.

Max leaned forward and his shoulder brushed

against hers as he rambled on about out-boxes, in-boxes, and signature lines. She loved having him near her. There was something about him that made her feel young and alive again. She never thought anyone would have ever taken the place of Marty, and in a real sense, no one ever could. But Max was different. Max was. . .Max. But while he was nothing like Marty, losing one husband made her extremely cautious about losing her heart again.

"Pricilla?"

Her gaze broke away from the screen that now was a mess of cold, sterile typing. "Sorry."

He sat back and caught her gaze. "Have you heard a word I've said?"

She offered him a weak smile. "I know that we can send e-mails, and you mentioned something about in-boxes and the Internet—"

"You'll catch on quickly. I promise." He was far too excited. "Now, look at this."

Thirty minutes later Pricilla rubbed her neck and tried to get rid of the crick that had started at the base of her skull and was now working its way down her spine. She'd tried her best to pay attention to Max's crash course she'd secretly nicknamed the World Wild Web 101, but she was afraid that the learning curve was too great. What was the old saying? You can't teach an old dog new tricks? Replace dogs and tricks with a sixty-five-year-old-grandma-wannabe and a state-of-the-art laptop, and you'd about have it right.

She stole a glance at Max and caught sight of his blue eyes. She'd always said they reminded her of the columbine in the spring. And they were smiling. Computers. . .Reggie Pierce's death. . .their uncertain relationship. . .nothing seemed to matter at the moment except for the fact that Max Summers was sitting beside her and he loved her. Even at sixty-five, he still had the same broad, strong shoulders and a military physique from frequent workouts. Seeing him was enough to make up for his wanting her to learn how to use a computer and send e-mails. Truth was she'd missed him.

". . .this is where you can organize messages. Save those you want to keep, or throw away those you don't need any longer."

Pricilla's gaze flicked back to the screen, and she forced herself to concentrate. After Charles Woodruff's death, Max had used her son's computer to research three of the suspects. What if she could do the same thing for the suspects in Reggie Pierce's case?

She stared at the emblems on the bottom of the screen. "Can I get on the Internet?"

"Good question." He smiled. No matter what the mirror told her every morning, she knew Max saw beyond her wrinkles and age spots. "All you have to do is click on this icon like this. Nathan's wireless system makes it easy. You can log on from anywhere in the lodge."

"Log on. . .icons. . .wireless—"

"You'll get the hang of it quickly." He squeezed her hand. "I promise."

Someone in high heels walked across the hardwood floor. Pricilla turned to see Annabelle in the doorway, her eyes puffy from lack of sleep.

Pricilla sat up straight. "Annabelle? I didn't hear you come in."

The woman clutched the doorframe and took a step back. "I'm sorry. You have company. I'll come back later—"

"No. It's fine." Pricilla stood and crossed the room

Annabelle grasped Pricilla's hands. "I. . .I need to talk."

With Max settled on the front porch with a crossword puzzle and a third helping of peach cobbler, Pricilla quickly fixed a pot of tea then joined Annabelle in the living room. It was the least she could do for the woman who had just lost her husband.

Annabelle stirred her drink then poured another spoonful of sugar in the cup before taking a sip. "I hardly know where to start. It's been almost a week, and I still keep thinking that I'm going to wake up and this will all be nothing but a bad dream."

"You've got to grieve and give it time." Pricilla put her used tea bag on an empty plate, wishing she could take away the woman's pain. "Healing will come eventually."

Annabelle gazed out the window. "We fought before he died, and the last words I said to him were horrible. I. . .I threatened to leave him."

Pricilla wasn't surprised at all. "Frankly, Reggie wasn't the easiest man to get along with. I certainly don't think you should blame yourself. I'm sure you had a good reason."

"But I loved him. I never would have left him."

Pricilla stared at the floral pattern on the delicate cup and saucer and bit her tongue. Subtlety wasn't exactly one of her strong suits, and speaking ill of Annabelle's dead husband, no matter how true, was wrong. Honestly. She knew better than that. "I'm sorry—"

"No, it's all right. I'm not blind to the fact that no one in town liked him."

"Reggie was simply a man who was. . ." Pricilla quickly searched for the right word, determined not to make the same mistake again. But what could she say that was both truthful and yet not condemning? Reggie had been demanding, difficult, and overbearing, and those three words barely began to describe the man.

Annabelle leaned back in her chair and ran her fingers through her short, curly hair. "I feel so guilty."

"Guilty?" The detective might be looking at motives for foul play, but Pricilla would never believe Annabelle had been involved in her husband's death. "Why?"

"I just wish things had been different." Annabelle wrung her hands. "I feel guilty that I didn't spend more time working on my marriage, or more time being a better wife. . . or more time being the spiritual example I should have been."

Even though Reggie had never entered a church building and had always seemed proud of the fact, Annabelle had never given up hope that her husband would one day understand why she believed as she did. But Pricilla was certain that her friend's faith had suffered because of it.

"I can't imagine that God. . ." Annabelle shook her head. "Why should God forgive me if Reggie couldn't?"

"Forgive you for what exactly?"

Before she could answer, the cell phone in Annabelle's purse rang. She pulled it out of the black bag. "Excuse me, if it's one of my children. . ."

Pricilla nodded as Annabelle mumbled a hello. While she didn't believe that Ezri or Stewart had enjoyed a healthy relationship with their father, the situation was still tragic.

Annabelle's face paled.

"What is it?" Pricilla set down her tea and leaned forward.

Annabelle clicked the phone shut. "It was Detective Carter. I think I've just become his number-one suspect."

5

Max flipped through the pages of his favorite hunting magazine while he waited for Pricilla, who sat beside him on the couch, to get off the phone. Normally, he would enjoy the full-page advertisement on the latest hunting gear, or the feature story on Alaska's big game, but this evening he found it hard to concentrate no matter how interesting the subject. He'd been right about Pricilla. Her success in solving the murder of Charles Woodruff was influencing the situation with Annabelle. Pricilla might say she had no intentions of getting involved, but he knew her better than that. Instead of dishing up a second helping of peach cobbler, he was afraid she was about to dish up a second helping of trouble.

He flicked on the small table lamp beside the leather couch he sat on and forced himself to read what he was sure would prove to be an informative article packed full of proven scouting tips. Within seconds the page became a blur. Pricilla's voice lowered beside him, then there was a long pause. He held his breath until she began talking again, but he couldn't make sense of the conversation.

Shoving the magazine into the rack beside him, he folded his arms across his chest and heaved a deep sigh. It wasn't as if he didn't trust Pricilla's instincts, because they were typically on target. Nor did he believe she was incapable of solving a crime—including Reggie

Pierce's. But murder was. . .well. . .murder, and he didn't want her involved.

The cozy living room, with its high ceiling and glossy wooden floors, reverberated with the sounds of a few lingering guests playing a lively game of cards, but he finally had to admit defeat and tuned out the murmurs of conversation interspersed with laughter to once again listen to Pricilla. The concern in her voice was what had him worried. She would never sit back and allow the detective—and a bumbling one at that in her opinion—do his job when she believed that justice wasn't being served. Her brief experience as an amateur detective last year had transformed her into a sixty-five-year-old investigator—enterprising, fearless, and out to save the world.

He lifted his head as the phone clicked shut.

Pricilla laid the phone on the end table and slid closer to him. "That was Annabelle."

"I figured as much." He was determined not to overreact, or nag, or any other number of things he longed to do. "Did she talk to the detective?"

"Yes, and it doesn't look good. I'm afraid her fear of being Detective Carter's number-one suspect isn't far from the truth." She shook her head, allowing a fringe of silver curls to bounce around the nape of her neck. "She's innocent, Max."

He wasn't convinced. "People have secrets, things that you might never even begin to guess—"

"I can't imagine Annabelle having a secret so shocking that she would murder her husband because of it." She caught his gaze and frowned. "We've become close friends during the past few months, and while she'd always hinted at unhappiness in her marriage, murder is a whole other thing."

"Perhaps."

With a cozy fire in the hearth to ward off the final chill of spring and soft music playing in the background, the last thing he wanted to do was argue. Or talk about Annabelle Pierce. His chief objective originally might have been to ensure Pricilla stayed out of trouble, but the truth was, he'd shown up on her doorstep for a much more significant reason. He had every intention of reviving their stagnant relationship. He'd missed her, and with marriage in the back of his mind, he knew it was time to begin courting again. First things first, though. "What did the detective say?"

Pricilla lowered her gaze and began picking at a chipped nail. "They found a new will Reggie presumably had typed up. It was unsigned and dated the day before he died. He cut both Annabelle and the children out of his will."

"Presumably." Max sucked in his breath. If Reggie had indeed written the will, it was definitely a motive for murder. "Had he threatened Annabelle with this information, or even told her about it?"

From the look on her face, Pricilla obviously realized how damaging the evidence was. "Yes, but she didn't believe he would actually go through with it. Reggie was a hard man to get along with. He always looked for leverage to get what he wanted. It's strange. Somehow, in spite of his cantankerous character, she still loved him."

Even Max couldn't help but feel sorry for the woman. "How's she doing?"

"Annabelle's a strong woman. It will take time, but I think she'll pull through."

Max drummed his fingers against the leather armrest. Maybe Pricilla was right. She was a good judge of character and was rarely wrong when it came to her gut instincts about people. But if Annabelle hadn't killed off her husband in a fit of rage, then who had?

Pricilla rested her hand against his arm. "I thought I would stop by the bakery tomorrow. To support the business, of course."

He definitely smelled an ulterior motive in this vein of the conversation. "Just for support?"

"If I happen to find out a clue relevant to the case, it would be wrong to dismiss it." She flashed him a pleading look that was going to get him in the end. "Annabelle can't afford to close down the bakery, and the sheriff told her that as long as the police have access to whatever they need, she'll be allowed to keep it running."

"So you'll just purchase a few dozen pastries and perhaps some of their baguettes?" He didn't buy her reasoning, but resisting her was impossible.

"Annabelle's a good friend, and I have to support her. Besides that, they have the most divine Italian shortbread cookies. You'd love them."

"After three helpings of your peach cobbler, I hardly think I need to indulge on shortbread." He patted his stomach and laughed. "I suppose a trip to the bakery wouldn't hurt anything, though I'm quite certain you're hoping to find more than just a sampling of pastries."

———

Pricilla eyed the assortment of pastries beneath the glass case and felt her mouth water. She'd definitely discovered one of her weaknesses. She could hardly resist driving by the quaint bakery without stopping in for a taste of a fresh fruit tart or perhaps a chocolate truffle, and today was no exception. The shopping list in her pocket crinkled between her fingers. Five long baguettes would never be enough. Of course, she could simply go to the grocery store to buy all the baguettes she needed, as well as get the ingredients to make tonight's dessert herself. She was quite adept at making her own delicious cakes and pastries, but then she might miss a chance to gather information on Reggie's death, which, besides supporting Annabelle's business, was the real reason she was here.

She turned to Max, who was drooling over a tray of almond cream pastries. "Would you like one?"

"One?" His gaze shifted to the cream horns. "How in the world would I ever choose just one? The selection is incredible."

"You can't. I've sampled all of them, and trust me, you can't go wrong with any of them." She laughed and hoped the indulgence didn't show too much on her waistline. "Reggie learned how to make pastries from a chef in Paris. Of course, now that Reggie's dead. . ."

Now that Reggie was dead what?

Annabelle relied on the income of the bakery to support her family. With two kids in college, finances had to be tight no matter how well the business was thriving. And then there was the added complication of the mail-order side of the company. Annabelle had always been highly involved in the business, and they had a full-time baker capable of keeping up with the demand, but if she were arrested for the murder of her husband that would change everything.

A cherry tart caught Pricilla's eye, but she forced herself to focus. Pastries and cream-filled cakes were not why she was here. She was here to help Annabelle find out who murdered her husband, and if that meant talking to employees, making phone calls, or even doing a bit of undercover sleuthing, she would do it.

She clicked her fingers against the glass and wondered why no one was working in the front. Everything in the store looked normal. The glass and chrome had been polished, the floor swept, and even the hand-painted OPEN sign hung in place out front. All as if nothing had changed. For a moment she expected Reggie to walk through the swinging wooden doors from the back with his gruff exterior and long apron covered in flour and smears of chocolate.

But of course he didn't.

A knot twisted inside Pricilla's stomach as she tried to block out the imprint of the last time she'd seen Reggie. Cold stone flooring. . .the shattered vase. . .his motionless body. . . At least she hadn't come alone this time. Max had agreed to accompany her to the bakery, mumbling some excuse about needing to get out of the house and into the fresh air, but his words didn't fool her. He was here to keep an eye on her. In fact, it wouldn't surprise her at all if her son had put him up to the idea. Honestly, how much trouble did they really think she could get into at a bakery—unless it had to do with consuming too many calories?

She stole a peek at Max's reflection in the glass and felt her heart trip. Part of her hoped she was wrong and that he had really come to Colorado to see her and not just to ensure she didn't try her hand at being Jessica Fletcher once again. He looked quite handsome in khaki pants and a checkered, button-down shirt. She couldn't help it. When Max was with her, fears about the future began to melt away along with all her excuses as to why a permanent relationship with him couldn't work.

Ezri stepped into the storefront from the backroom, forcing Pricilla once again to concentrate on the issue at hand. The young woman's neon orange outfit did little to perk up the somber expression on her face.

She ran her hand through her cropped hair. "Mrs. Crumb, I'm so sorry I kept you waiting. I was filling an order in the back. We're a bit understaffed today."

"I know this is a hard time for you, but it's good to see you." Pricilla set her purse on the counter and gave her a reassuring smile. "I thought perhaps you might be closing early for the day?"

The young woman shook her head. "Mother insists we need to keep the store open."

Pricilla tugged Max toward the counter. "I'd like to introduce you to Max Summers. He's a good friend of mine."

"It's nice to meet you." Ezri cocked her head and stared at him. "You're Mr. Summers? Trisha's father?"

"Yes. Do you know her?"

For the first time, Ezri's face lit up. "She's such a sweet person. She comes in from time to time and always orders one Napoleon and one lemon tart."

Max smiled. "I'd forgotten those are her favorites. She's always had a sweet tooth."

"She's told me what a great dad she has. It's nice to meet you in person." Ezri's gaze clouded over.

Max took a step forward. "I'm so sorry about what happened to your father, Ezri."

"Unfortunately, my father and I were never close. Business always came first for him." She held up her hand as if to dismiss in one sweep all the pent-up pain and rejection she felt. "Anyway, it's really good to meet you."

"It's nice to meet you, too."

Pricilla pulled out her wallet. "We thought we'd stir up a bit of business for you. I need five baguettes and two dozen of your individual meringue-almond cakes."

"Mmm, these are one of my favorites." Ezri pulled out a white box and began filling it with a layer of the round cakes. "I'm sure your guests will enjoy them."

"Speak for yourself." Max now had his sights on a row of walnut puffs. "Who says I'm going to let Pricilla share them with our guests?"

If it was true that the way to a man's heart was through his stomach, Pricilla had certainly knocked on the right door. "I'm convinced I've inhaled at least a thousand calories just by standing here."

Ezri laughed, but the sound rang hollow. Pricilla couldn't help but remember the incident in the parking lot the day of the funeral. Ezri's expression had bothered her that day, and if her assumptions were correct, the girl was still worried about something.

"What is it, Ezri? You look. . .scared."

Ezri glanced toward the back room before reaching for another meringue-almond cake with a pair of tongs. "It's nothing. Really."

"I might not know you well, but I do know your mother, and I'm concerned for all of you."

Ezri set the box on the counter and stared at the speckled Formica top. "I don't know if I should say anything, Mrs. Crumb."

Pricilla ignored Max's disapproving look and continued. "I know your mother and that she could never be involved, but we need to find some sort of evidence to the contrary. If you know something—anything that might help—you can tell me."

Ezri leaned forward, sending Pricilla a strong whiff of the girl's perfume. "Part of the problem is Detective Carter. I know it's his job, but the detective is constantly snooping around and asking questions."

"What kind of questions?"

"For one, he's been grilling all the employees, which I can understand, but it's just the way he goes about it." She tugged at the bottom of her shirt. "He gives me the creeps."

Pricilla shot Max a look of triumph. She obviously wasn't the only one who found the detective's tactics both irritating and unprofessional. "And. . ."

"Well, Darren Robinson is a college student my dad hired for the summer. He's really good at computers and has been updating the bakery's Web sites and doing other things that will boost the mail-order business." Ezri shivered despite the warmth in the storefront. "He's a nice enough guy, who keeps to himself, but. . ."

Pricilla pressed against the counter to ensure she didn't miss anything. "Do you think he had something to do with your father's death?"

"Not Darren, but what worries me is what he told the detective. He said he saw Stewart on the balcony moments before my dad died. He was standing behind the pot and looking down on the patio." Tears welled up in Ezri's eyes. "I just don't think Mom could handle the fact that Stewart may have been involved."

Pricilla didn't like what she was hearing, but at the same time, she was quite certain that dropping a heavy pot from a balcony would never be Stewart's modus operandi. The boy was studying forensic science. Certainly if he'd wanted to kill his father, he would have come up with something a bit more scientific, wouldn't he? Still, such reasoning wasn't enough to dismiss the young man as a suspect.

"Do you think your brother is capable of murder?"

Ezri shrugged a shoulder. "I won't lie. Stewart is a lot like my dad was when it comes to living the good life. He wants to live it up without any of the responsibility and doesn't want to hear you say it won't work."

"Maybe I could talk to him."

Max finally spoke up again. "I'm sure the detective has done that, Pricilla."

"He did." Ezri grabbed five of the wrapped baguettes, placed them on the counter, and began ringing up the sale. "But Stewart isn't talking much to anyone right now, and I doubt you'd be any different."

Pricilla knew Max wouldn't approve of her next question, but she asked it anyway. "Do you know where your brother is right now?"

Ezri shrugged. "I know where he's supposed to be. In the back, filling orders from our Web site. Instead, he's probably down at the pool hall."

Stewart wasn't at the pool hall as Ezri had predicted. Pricilla swallowed her disappointment and followed Max past a vintage photo shop, a travel agent, and a gift shop as they walked toward the car.

"It's just as well," he told her. "I hardly think that the pool hall is an appropriate place for either of us."

She swallowed her frustration. "This is Rendezvous, Max. Not Las Vegas."

"True, but—"

"Wait a minute." Pricilla stopped just past the corner drugstore where the street opened up to the town park. "There he is."

Stewart sat on one of the wrought iron benches, his hands stuffed inside his jacket pockets, simply staring across the empty playground. Dark, unruly hair that needed a good haircut. A red T-shirt and shorts that looked as if they'd been slept in for the past week. Pricilla tossed the baguettes onto the backseat of the car and tried to come up with an opening line that would get him to talk. She couldn't imagine the three of them having many shared interests, but there had to be at least one common denominator.

Annabelle's plea for help replayed in her mind. Until the truth behind Reggie's death was revealed, Annabelle wouldn't be able to go on with her life. It was enough to propel Priscilla down the cobblestone walk toward the young man. With a new wave of determination and a box of meringue-almond cakes, Pricilla hurried toward Stewart.

"Pricilla, wait." Max sped to catch up with her.

"I know what you're going to say." She turned to face him with the box of cakes against her chest. "And you have every right."

Max closed his mouth.

He obviously thought she agreed with his hesitation to grill Stewart, but she wasn't ready to completely concede. "All I want to do is ask him a couple questions."

"A couple questions?"

"If nothing else, he's Annabelle's son and it would be rude not to express my condolences."

Pricilla knew he didn't buy her reasoning, but it was the best she could come up with at the moment. And besides that, it really was true. She hadn't had the chance to talk with Stewart at the funeral and tell him how sorry she was for his loss.

"Please, Max."

"Just be careful. If he is the murderer. . ."

"He's Annabelle's son."

"Which doesn't make him innocent, and you know it."

She approached the young man from the side. "Stewart?"

There was no reaction.

Max pointed to the pair of earphones.

Pricilla slid into the space beside Stewart. According to Nathan, the park had been constructed five years ago. The surrounding mountains, with a dusting of snow along the top, made the spot a perfect photo op. But Pricilla had her doubts that Stewart noticed any of it. And since talking wasn't getting his attention, she hoped the fresh pastries would. She opened the lid of the box of still warm cakes and waited a few seconds for the warm scent of almonds to fill the air.

Stewart turned then pulled the earphones out. "Mrs. Crumb. . .and Mr. . . ."

Max stood in front of them, looking almost as uncomfortable as Stewart did. "Summers. Max Summers."

Stewart nodded.

Pricilla waited a few more seconds. "Would you like a cake? They're fresh from the oven."

He shrugged.

She'd obviously taken him off guard, which might be a good thing. Pricilla decided to seize the opportunity. She handed him one of the cakes. "I'd be ten pounds lighter if it weren't for your father's bakery."

Pricilla frowned as he shoved a bite in his mouth.

That wasn't at all what she'd intended to say. Ezri had said he didn't talk much, and now he had an excuse. The last thing the boy wanted, she was sure, was yet another reminder of his father's death.

She cleared her throat. She might as well get the condolence part over with so she could find some less shaky ground between them. "What I really wanted to say was that I haven't had a chance to tell you how sorry I am about your father's death. I know this is a very difficult time for you."

Stewart shrugged again before taking another bite. This was going to be harder than she thought. If she, of all people, couldn't start a conversation, she wasn't sure who could.

"So you think I killed my father?" His words were somewhat garbled with a mouthful of meringue. But not so garbled that she couldn't understand.

"I certainly didn't say that."

"You didn't have to." He brushed the crumbs from the edges of his mouth and stood. "I know what people are thinking in this small town. I'm the prodigal son who didn't want to come home. Everyone knows about the fight I had with my dad the morning he died."

"I did hear that there had been some problems—"

"Did my mom also tell you that he was planning to cut me out of the will?"

"Well. . ."

Stewart's laugh rang hollow. "So I have the perfect motive."

"Stewart."

"And don't forget opportunity. Darren can place me at the scene of the crime moments before the actual murder."

She hadn't expected the boy to practically confess to a crime before she'd even asked her questions. "None of that means you killed your father."

"Doesn't it? The detective is pretty convinced. I've seen the look on his face. Even my mother has doubts of my innocence."

"Your mother loves you."

Stewart didn't reply.

"Do you want to tell me about the fight you had with your dad?" Pricilla prodded.

To her surprise, Stewart sat back down beside her. She offered him another almond cake, and he took it. The features on his face softened. He was nothing more than a confused adolescent with some growing up to do. The murder of his father, no matter where their relationship stood, had to have put a kink in the process.

Max moved to the other side of the bench and sat without saying a word.

"My father and I never got along. He was always busy with work. Too busy to attend little league games and track meets."

Pricilla bit the edge of her lip to refrain from making a comment. There was no doubt that the boy needed to talk. If she interrupted at this point she'd probably lose her advantage.

"In New York he had his restaurant," Stewart continued. "It was like his first-born son. It got all his attention. When they decided to move here, my mom promised me things would be different. I believed her at first. The only thing was, school holidays are also peak times for the store. So when I was home from college, I worked."

Stewart fiddled with the white cord of his headphones. "The morning he was murdered, my father told me that I was nothing more than a lazy bum who didn't deserve a dime of his hard-earned money. I told him I didn't want any of it, slammed the door, and walked out of the house. Some of his last words to me were that he was cutting me out of his will. I wasn't surprised. He loved to dictate my life but never took the time to really know what I wanted." He slapped his hands against his thighs. "At least everybody's happy now. The town has the perfect scapegoat, saving its touristy image, and the detective can put another star on his badge for another solved murder."

"If the detective had any real evidence that you'd killed your father, he'd have already arrested you," Pricilla insisted. "I've worked with the man before, and while it's true he can be quite blunt, I think it's mainly because he's motivated to do his job and keep this community safe." Pricilla couldn't believe she was defending the detective, but if digging out a few morsels of truth helped reassure Stewart, it was worth it. "I don't think he'd ever do anything to hurt you on purpose."

"Tell that to yourself next time you're hauled down to the sheriff's office in front of your friends for a couple hours of questioning. I'll bet you'll think plenty different."

She had no intention of getting hauled down to the sheriff's office for any reason, but she did understand his point.

Stewart shook his head and frowned. The hard lines that had creased his forehead earlier returned. The moment of confession was over.

Pricilla closed the lid of the bakery box and considered Stewart's words. She wasn't convinced yet of his guilt but still needed to ask one more question. And since he seemed to be playing things straight, so would she. "Did you kill your father, Stewart?"

Stewart shoved his hands back into his pockets and rose to leave. "Since you seem so keen on playing the role of detective, why don't you figure that out yourself?"

Pricilla breathed in the aroma of the fresh bakery items that sat behind her in the car and kept her eyes on the winding road that led back to the lodge.

Max had taken exactly thirty seconds once they were back in the car to dive into the box of pastries to ensure they were suitable for the guests. Or so he claimed. "So what are you thinking?" she asked.

He took another bite. "How glad I am that you didn't give all these pastries to Stewart. It's got to be one of the most divine pastries I've ever tasted. Besides yours, of course—"

"I wasn't talking about almond cream and apricot fillings." Pricilla couldn't help but laugh. "And there's a glob of something at the corner of your mouth."

Max quickly wiped it away before finishing the last bite.

She slowed down to turn the corner on to the road that led to the lodge. "I was referring to our talk with Ezri, Darren's claim of seeing Stewart at the crime scene moments before Reggie's untimely death, our unexpected talk with Stewart. . .all of it."

"What am I thinking?" He closed the lid of the box, keeping his promise to only sample one, and set it on the backseat next to the other groceries they'd picked up. "The exact same thing as when you thought you'd murdered Charles Woodruff with one of your salmon-filled tartlets. I think you need to let the detective handle things."

"What if he arrests the wrong person?"

"You worry too much."

Only with good reason. "Would you trust the detective if it were your neck on the line?"

The pregnant pause that followed gave ample clue as to what he was about to say. Max cleared his throat. "Let's just say I'm glad I'm not in the position to find out."

Pricilla rolled down her window a couple inches. While there was a place for air conditioners, there was nothing like breathing in the fresh mountain air in springtime. "You must have an opinion about Stewart. You saw the boy. If you ask me, he's simply hurting over his father's death, which is a different emotion altogether from guilt. I don't think Stewart Pierce killed his father."

"While you might be right, he does have both

motive and means. And there was a lot of anger in that boy that even you can't deny."

"True, but a lot of people get angry without unleashing their anger in the form of a crime."

"Sometimes all it takes is one pivotal moment to prove what's really inside a person. For the good and for the bad."

"That's a bit negative, don't you think?"

"God created man to be complex and to make his own decisions." Max opened the lid of the pastry box. "That's what makes us unique."

"What am I going to feed my guests tonight?"

"Stewart had two."

"I needed something to keep the boy talking." She shot him a grin. "What if I promise to make cinnamon rolls for you in the morning?"

He smiled and flipped the lid shut. There was no doubt that the way to Max's heart was through his stomach. And she supposed he had a point about the complexity of man, but she preferred to look at the situation in a less philosophical manner.

The lodge came into view. Nathan and Trisha stood on the porch and waved.

"At least we have something to celebrate in the midst of all this. Now all we need is for Nathan to finally pop the question."

Which made her feel a bit guilty about being happy over her son's relationship with Trisha when Annabelle was still in mourning. But not enough to completely douse the joy she felt over possible upcoming nuptials between the two. She'd seen the changes in Nathan.

Trisha's move to Rendezvous so they could give their relationship a go was the best thing that had happened in as long as she could remember.

Pricilla pulled into the drive and parked the car then adjusted her bifocals. Trisha had a tissue in her hand. "Max, she looks as if she's been crying."

With her arms filled with baguettes, Pricilla got out of the car and hurried up the front steps. Max followed close behind with the pastries and the rest of the groceries. All she needed was another disaster to strike. Dealing with the aftereffects of Reggie's death gave her enough to fret over. Trisha blew her nose and leaned against the railing. The young woman's normally stunning eyes were red and puffy. If something was wrong with her. . .or if Nathan had broken up with her. . .well, her son would never hear the end of it. She adored Trisha, and it was high time her son got married and produced a grandchild.

Nathan took the pile of baguettes and motioned toward the front door. "Would the two of you mind coming inside? Trisha and I will put the groceries away then meet you in the living room. We have something to tell you."

6

Pricilla sat on the edge of the couch beside Max and braced herself for the bad news. While she didn't want to jump to conclusions, the clues all led to the same place. Trisha had been crying, and now the couple had something to tell her and Max. She could think of only one scenario that included Trisha crying and both Nathan and Trisha insisting on talking to the two of them together.

Nathan and Trisha were breaking up.

The very idea sent a band of shivers up her spine and turned her stomach sour. How could Nathan even consider such a thing? He'd finally found the perfect woman—thanks to his mother, she might add—but now, for some lame reason, he was ready to throw it all away?

The first time she'd met Trish, she knew that the young woman was ideal for her son. Not only was she smart, extremely attractive, and a Christian, she was single. That singleness, though, hadn't taken long to change once Pricilla had put her matchmaking skills into play. Trisha Summers was simply everything Pricilla had imagined in a daughter-in-law. And she had no intention of losing the girl.

She dug her nails into the arm of the couch. "I think Nathan and Trisha are breaking up."

"Breaking up?" The statement obviously caught Max off guard. "I can't imagine that. I don't ever remember seeing Trisha happier than she is now."

"I know she's been happy with Nathan, but something's wrong." Pricilla fiddled with the fringe on a throw pillow and wished she had something productive to do with her hands. She'd never been good at simply sitting. And waiting was even worse. "Didn't you notice she's been crying?"

Max continued thumbing through a hunting magazine. "She told me last night she thought she was coming down with a cold. I gave her some of my vitamin C tablets, and she went to bed early."

Pricilla still wasn't convinced that a lack of vitamins was Trisha's only problem. "What if my son has come down with a case of cold feet and has called things off between them?"

"It certainly wouldn't be the first time a couple broke up, but I think you're worrying over nothing." Max set down the magazine and gave her his full attention. "And speaking of doubts, I've been thinking a lot about you and me lately. I know this isn't the time for me to bring this up, but it seems to me that a case of cold feet might apply in our relationship as well."

Pricilla grimaced at the sting of his words, but only because she knew they were true. While neither of them had made the offer to move and change their relationship from a long-distance one to one where they actually lived in the same county, she had been the one who pulled back every time the subject of something permanent was broached.

It wasn't as if she didn't love Max or that she didn't enjoy his company. Far from it. Even now, his presence brought her a sense of security and stability. But what if that wasn't enough?

She knew that when he left to go back to New Mexico in a few days, the same fears would surface. Once, she'd thought it would just be a matter of time before she could shove her doubts aside. Doubts that she could truly find love the second time around. Doubts that at sixty-five she would be able to—or simply willing to—make the necessary adjustments. Doubts that she would be able to get over a second broken heart if something were to happen to Max.

More and more she wasn't so sure.

Even so, being afraid of losing Max like she'd lost Marty seemed a lame excuse. She'd never give up the forty-three years she'd had with her first husband in order to have saved her heart when he died. So why was making things permanent with Max any different? He was the best thing in her life right now, and she knew she'd be a fool to give him up.

"Max, I just don't—"

Trisha and Nathan entered the room then sat across from her and Max, leaving Max's comment hanging. For now, anyway. She knew it would only be a matter of time before the issue came up again.

Trisha blew her nose as tears formed in the corners of her eyes. Whatever the future held between her and Max, Pricilla couldn't stand the thought of her son breaking Trisha's heart.

Pricilla furrowed her brow. "How could you, Nathan?"

Her son shot her a blank look. "How could I what?"

"Look at her. She's crying."

"Crying? No." Trisha gave her a faint smile then blew her nose again. "Allergies. I'm absolutely miserable."

"Allergies?" Pricilla felt a wave of relief wash over her. "Why, that's wonderful."

"Wonderful?" Nathan wrapped his arm about Trisha and pulled her close.

"I didn't mean wonderful as in I'm-glad-you're-not-feeling-well. Not at all. I simply meant. . ."

Pricilla huffed out a deep sigh. Why did she always manage to get herself into such embarrassing messes? Jumping to conclusions. . .overlooking crucial pieces of evidence. . .and most importantly, allowing her fears to take over. Some detective she was. The entire thing was really Reggie Pierce's fault. If he hadn't gone and gotten himself murdered, she wouldn't be trying to turn every situation into an investigation. She glanced at Max, who, instead of coming to her rescue, seemed just as ready for an explanation.

Pricilla offered them all a weak smile. "Trisha looked as if she was crying, so first thing of course I imagined was that the two of you had broken things off."

"Quite the opposite, Mom."

Nathan held out Trisha's left hand. Pricilla's eyes widened. How in the world had she missed such a stunning ring? The diamond had to be at least half a karat.

"Trisha and I are engaged."

"Engaged?" Max broke into a grin. "Congratulations!"

Pricilla flew across the thick area rug to gather her son and future daughter-in-law into her arms. She might actually get the chance to hold her grandbabies before they sent her away to an old age home after all.

～

Max watched Pricilla out of the corner of his eye while she rambled on to Trisha about wedding dresses and colors. He was definitely going to have his work cut out for him in the coming weeks.

He caught snippets of the conversation between giggles and laughter. *Wedding planners. . .antique lace. . . no reason to wait too long. . .*

No reason to wait too long.

He might not know a thing about invitation etiquette and caterers, but that one phrase stuck with him. He'd sensed Pricilla's hesitation in their own relationship, and even though he realized they still had a number of obstacles standing between them, he truly wanted things to work out. When she'd flown down to see him in February, he'd considered proposing, but somehow she'd always managed to steer the subject away from anything permanent. To him, it was clear. For whatever reason, Pricilla wasn't ready to take the next step. And while he knew he loved her, he also knew that he wasn't content to wait indefinitely for her to decide what she wanted.

～

Even though she'd slept restlessly the night before, Pricilla still rose before the sun managed to make an appearance above the horizon. By nine o'clock she'd fed all the guests a hearty breakfast of scrambled eggs, biscuits and gravy, bacon, hash browns, and blueberry muffins, chatted with Trisha about a local florist when she dropped Max off at the lodge, and set up a tour of the bakery for half past ten with Annabelle. If she was to discover any new insights into Reggie's case—especially certain noteworthy details the pushy detective might overlook—meeting Annabelle's employees was essential.

Max wandered into the kitchen with a crossword puzzle in one hand and an empty coffee mug in the other. How could his eyes, ones that reminded her of Frank Sinatra, and his cologne, which always left her head reeling, leave her breathless one minute and ready to run away the next? She couldn't forget his comment from yesterday, and even after tossing and turning all night she still wasn't ready to respond to it. Even so, her stomach flipped as Max, wearing his worn loafers, shot her a grin before moving silently across the kitchen to refill his coffee from the coffeepot.

Watching him out of the corner of her eye, she stirred the stew she'd made for today's lunch and wished she had a clear response for him. She'd written down a dozen excuses in her journal last night, but that's all that they had been, excuses. Funny. She'd never before been accused of having cold feet—especially considering she normally jumped into things rather than stopping to examine the consequences—but for some reason love had tangled up her emotions and brought about the most unexpected reaction: a case of cold feet as difficult to unravel as the case of their local dead baker.

Turning down the stove a notch, she waited until Max was finished doctoring his drink before speaking. "I feel as if I owe you an apology for yesterday."

"An apology?" He took a sip then wrapped his hands around the hot mug. Even with spring in the air, the morning still had a slight chill. "What for?"

"For being the one with cold feet in this relationship. For not knowing where we're going, or even where I want things to go."

His gaze never left her face. "You don't owe me an apology. I shouldn't have broached the subject like that."

She wiped her hands on her apron before covering the bowl of coleslaw with plastic wrap and putting it in the refrigerator. "You were right. I have been hesitant to let our relationship go ahead, and I'm not even sure why. When you're here, I feel young again, and when you're away, I miss you, but it's hard to stay truly connected only through phone calls and letters."

She eyed the laptop on the dining room table. He had promised more lessons today, but she was quite certain that even daily e-mails would never take the place of face-to-face contact. In order for things to work between them, something was going to have to change. But she wasn't sure she was willing to pack up her life and move to New Mexico. Even for Max.

"Part of the problem, I'm sure, is that living so far apart simply isn't conducive to a growing relationship." Max leaned against the granite counter. "And I admit that I've been just as stubborn at the thought of moving here."

"It's completely understandable considering the fact that you've lived in New Mexico your entire life. You're a leader in the church and in the community—"

"The very same reasons I can't ask you to leave here. And besides that, I haven't seen you so happy since before Marty died."

Max's statement simply confirmed what she'd been feeling. She was happy here and had seen the thought of moving to New Mexico as a choice between doing something she loved, and finding love.

He bridged the gap between them and took her hand. "Like it or not, we're no longer two naïve teen-agers ready to step out together and face the world. We've already faced many of the ups and downs of life head-on, which tends to give us a completely different outlook. And there's something else I think we're both forgetting. I realized yesterday that we've been going about this relationship all wrong."

"What do you mean?"

He squeezed her hand. "We need to pray about our relationship, Pricilla. It's something I admit that I haven't done nearly as much as I should have. I don't know. Maybe you're not the only one with cold feet."

Pricilla pressed her lips together. It was one thing for her to have cold feet, but for him to have them as well... She sighed. Of course he was right. How had she managed to spend time trying to convince Annabelle to keep praying and to give her loss to Christ, yet had rarely taken time to bathe her own relationship with Max in prayer?

It was time she laid it all before her heavenly Father. "It's interesting how you can give advice on how to give it all to God, but when it comes to putting that advice into practice yourself, it often gets lost in the bustle of life."

"Like with Annabelle?"

Pricilla nodded. "I've been trying to encourage her to not give up and to let God be her source of strength, but she feels guilty over Reggie's death."

"Guilty?"

"Guilty that she didn't work harder to make things work between them." Pricilla paused, startled at the correlation to her own life. Was she going to feel guilty one day for letting a second chance for love pass her by because she was afraid, or perhaps unwilling to take a chance?

Max shoved his now cold coffee into the microwave. "What did Paul say in 2 Corinthians? 'We are hard pressed on every side but not crushed'?"

Pricilla nodded. She knew the verse well. "And 'struck down, but not destroyed.'"

Walking through difficulties was never easy. She watched Max grab the last blueberry muffin from the serving plate then take a bite while he waited for his coffee to finish heating up. Part of her longed for more intimate moments like this. Moments when she could bask in the familiarity of the two of them together. Conversations in the kitchen. . .over breakfast. . . perhaps under a starlit sky. Surely this was something she could get used to again.

The microwave beeped and Max took the mug back out. "I overheard you talking with Annabelle this morning. How is she?"

"About the same. Still trying to find her footing in all of this. I told her I'd stop by this morning. She's going to give me a tour of the bakery."

"Along with a chance to cross-examine the employees?" Max's eyebrows rose while she tried to ignore the unasked questions.

"You wouldn't mind if I happened to stop and chat with some of the employees, would you?"

"And if I did, would that make any difference?"

She caught the teasing in his voice despite his serious expression. "I—"

"I'm sorry." He winked at her. "Admittedly, that was an unfair question. I'll come along if I can play Watson on this quest."

She smiled, relieved that he had agreed to come with her, even if it was only to keep an eye on her. "Of course you can, Doctor."

Pricilla dropped the lid onto the pot to let the stew simmer. It was amazing how a brand-new day—and talking with Max—made it easier to put things in a different perspective. She'd been foolish to worry over Trisha and Nathan's relationship, and perhaps she was foolish to worry about her own relationship with Max as well. Obviously, the stress over finding Reggie's body and the subsequent concern for Annabelle were taking their toll. As grateful as she was to Max for humoring her on her quest to see what she could find out at the bakery, she knew that his unspoken concerns to stay out of it had validity. What right did she have to overstep Detective Carter's authority in the case, no matter what her personal feelings were regarding the man? The very fact that she'd solved one investigation didn't mean she'd have the same success with Reggie's case.

But Annabelle had asked for her help, and for Pricilla, that was all the motivation she needed.

Max followed Pricilla and Annabelle through the back room of the bakery, surprised at how interesting the tour had been. Of course, part of his interest might be due to the variety of samples they'd been offered. Top of the list so far was the strawberry cream cheese tart that would force him to double his normal daily workout, but it had been a sacrifice well worth it.

Annabelle signaled them both to follow her to where a man was pulling a long pan of tart shells from the oven. "I know you wanted to meet our staff. I'll have to hire at least two more full-time workers in the next few weeks, but for now I want you to meet José, who's our incredible chef, as I'm sure you both can testify to. Reggie might have taught him everything he knows, but the man is also extremely talented. I'm not sure what I would do without him."

As soon as the chef had set down the tray, Pricilla stretched out her hand to greet him. "It's nice to meet you, José. We're regular customers of the bakery."

The man nodded but avoided Pricilla's gaze, something that didn't stop her from continuing. "How long have you lived in Rendezvous?"

"Six years."

"You must have known Mr. Pierce well, then."

"He was a fair boss who taught me well." No sign of bitterness was reflected in the man's eyes as he spoke.

Annabelle nodded across the room at a second man who could have been José's twin with his short stature, dark hair, and narrow eyes. "His brother Naldo works primarily in filling orders for our online business, where, as you already know, we ship our products all over the country."

Naldo nodded but didn't move from where he stood assembling packages of bakery items to be mailed. Neither man appeared inclined to talk, let alone succumb to an unscheduled cross-examination by an amateur detective.

A timer went off and José jumped. "I'm sorry, but if you'll excuse me. . ."

"Of course." Annabelle turned as another man entered the warm back room of the bakery. "And this is Darren Robinson, computer geek extraordinaire—his words, not mine—but I must agree, as he's quadrupled our business with our new Web site and other ideas, like using the bakery here as a test market for our products."

The phone rang in the corner of the room that had been partitioned off into a small office. Annabelle took a step toward the metal desk that was piled with folders. "I'm expecting a phone call from my estate attorney and need to answer that. Darren, if you wouldn't mind filling our guests in on some of the details of the mail-order side of the business, I'd appreciate it."

With a nod from Darren, Annabelle's heels clicked across the tile flooring as she hurried to pick up the phone.

Darren clasped his hands together and gave them a lopsided grin. "Is there anything in particular you'd like to know, Mrs. Crumb?"

Max looked at Pricilla, knowing exactly what questions she'd like to ask. Without a badge, though, her line of questioning was limited. A blessing, from his point of view.

Pricilla flashed Darren a smile. "It sounds as if you're quite the computer expert."

A slight blush crept up the young man's cheeks. "I've been teased a time or two that I'd rather hang out with my Intel Xeon than—"

"Your what?" Pricilla shook her head.

"My computer."

"Oh—"

"And why not? The information and possibilities are endless. Give me a little bit of time, and I can tell you where you went to college, which credit cards you own, and where you took your last vacation."

This time Pricilla stood speechless, and Max forced himself not to chuckle out loud. "Didn't I tell you a computer would be useful?"

Pricilla cleared her throat. "Can you really do all those things?"

"Well, at the very least, I can probably find out where you went to college and if you have a blog or a MySpace account online—"

"A blog?" Pricilla was definitely out of her territory this time. "Never mind. But I do have a question for you."

Darren shoved his hands into his jeans pockets and shrugged. "Shoot."

"Do you give lessons?"

"Lessons?" The young man reached up to push his thick glasses up the bridge of his nose.

"Computer lessons. I have a new one, but unfortunately I'm quite illiterate when it comes to electronic things." Her gaze shifted briefly to Max. "I know nothing about blogs or any of that, but I am particularly interested in learning how to use the Internet."

Max recognized exactly where her line of questioning was heading, and he wasn't sure he liked it. Still, what better way to find out everything she could about Reggie and the other suspects? "I didn't know you were so interested, Pricilla."

She shot him a knowing look. "It is the wave of the future."

Ten minutes later they were heading out the bakery's driveway with a computer lesson lined up for the following week.

Pricilla turned on her blinker and waited for a family of tourists to pass in front of them before merging onto Main Street. "Did you notice anything about José?"

"Besides the fact that he makes some of the best tarts I've ever tasted?"

She frowned, obviously not in the mood for jokes. "Yes, besides that fact."

"Then no."

"He seemed very nervous, and his gaze kept shifting."

"He's a chef who makes a mean strawberry tart."

Pricilla sucked in her breath. "There he is again."

She slammed on the brakes, and Max's hands hit the dashboard with a thud.

"Ouch! What are you talking about?"

"In the rearview mirror. It's the stranger who fought with Ezri the day of the funeral." She pulled the car against the curb, this time slowing to a stop. "He came out of the alley beside the bakery. I think it's time to add another suspect to my list."

7

Almost a week later, Pricilla finished frosting the last section of the cake then licked what was left of the lemon icing off the spatula. The sweet taste seemed a sharp contrast to her sour mood. Five days had passed since her unsuccessful visit to the bakery, where she'd learned nothing more than the fact that José and Naldo were nervous types (suspicious behavior perhaps, but not a valid reason to suspect them for murder), and that Darren was a computer wiz, which certainly wasn't a crime either. Even adding a seventh possible suspect had rendered no further evidence toward the truth. So, in regard to her investigation, she'd accomplished nothing.

Conversely, over the weekend the detective had taken in Annabelle for another round of questioning with the claims that forensics had uncovered further proof that foul play had been involved in Reggie's death. While no arrests had yet been made, or any details revealed, Annabelle had called Pricilla yesterday morning, certain that at any moment the detective would arrive at her doorstep with a warrant in his hands.

Something still didn't seem right in Pricilla's mind, and after their talk, she was even more convinced that Annabelle was innocent. But she hadn't been able to put her finger on the missing piece. Mulling over the list of suspects had done nothing more than leave her eyes blurred with fatigue and her brain refusing to cooperate.

As had the suspects themselves. Attempts to talk to Stewart on Friday at the bakery had left her with nothing more than an impression of an immature boy who needed a sense of direction in his life—but no signs of a murderer. Ezri was hiding something, Pricilla was certain, but she had a feeling it had nothing to do with her father's death and everything to do with her seventh suspect. That brought her back around to the bakery's two nervous employees and Darren the computer wiz. At least she still had her computer lesson with Darren in two days, but she was beginning to wonder if that, too, would lead to yet another dead end. With the progress she was making, she was liable to have more luck figuring out how to maneuver through the intricacies of the World Wide Web than making a breakthrough in the mystery surrounding Reggie's death. Stumbling across Charles Woodruff's murderer last October had obviously had nothing to do with her brilliant investigative skills, but instead had simply been a matter of luck.

Pricilla covered the cake before crossing out the last item on her to-do list for the lodge and glanced at the clock that hung on the wall. No matter what her frustrations over the case, she knew that Reggie's death and Annabelle's potential conviction weren't the real source of her restlessness. In less than thirty minutes, she would drive Max to the airport to catch his flight back to New Mexico. Instead of the sense of relief she thought she'd have, the very idea of his leaving left her feeling emptier than she'd ever imagined.

After his suggestion that she had cold feet, she'd decided that she needed time to not only pray about their relationship but time to step back and think about it—with Max on the other side of the state line. But in spite of her decision, the past week had been one of those nostalgic times she knew she would file in the recesses of her memory and pull out on a rainy day to savor.

He'd taken her out for dinner twice, to church on Sunday, and for a long drive into the mountains where they'd gone sightseeing like a couple of tourists. Even so, between wedding plans for Nathan and Trisha and late night Scrabble games, he'd avoided any further discussion of their future. The only thing that had been resolved between them had been their decision to pray about the situation until they saw each other again. And while prayer was definitely a step in the right direction, it had yet to clarify for her which direction her heart wanted their relationship to go.

Ignoring thoughts of cold feet versus lifelong commitment, Pricilla pulled a small notebook and pencil from the pocket of her sweater, for once thankful that she had something to think about besides Max. She'd compiled a list of suspects with as many details as she could, such as their links to the crime, motive, and opportunity. Filling in opportunity had been easy. All seven of her suspects had opportunity, except for perhaps Ezri's mystery man. Motives, on the other hand, had been harder to decipher. Even with her outspoken methods and candid questions, she'd discovered nothing that led to intent.

Max stepped into the kitchen set his suitcase on the floor, and laid his carry-on bag on the table, interrupting her train of thought. "Are you about ready to go?"

Pricilla flipped the notebook shut and shoved it in her pocket before turning around to face him. Blue eyes. . . broad shoulders. . .and that smile. Since when had the option of doing something she loved and choosing love ever been an issue in the first place? Especially with Max involved. Somehow love was never that simple.

She cleared her throat. "Yes, I was just. . .just making sure everything was ready for lunch."

"And the notebook?"

A wave of awkwardness rolled through the warmth of the kitchen. The sweet scent of lemons mingled with the chowder simmering on the stove, yet did nothing to whet her appetite.

Max had told her that he'd come to the same conclusion regarding Annabelle's innocence, but that left him worried that the real murderer was still lurking about. He wasn't happy with Pricilla's quest to find the truth, especially since he was leaving. "You promised me you would let the detective handle the case."

"I promised not to do anything foolish that would land me in jail—"

"Or in the morgue. There's a killer on the loose. . . remember." Max held up his hand and sighed. "I'm sorry. I'm not going to be here much longer, so let's promise that there will be no more talk of Reggie, or sleuthing, or suspects—"

"Or Detective Carter."

"Definitely not him." He returned her smile, making her heart ache all the more.

There was no doubt about it. She was going to have to make a decision. And soon.

An hour later Max stood at the airport window and watched Pricilla drive away, afraid he'd just made the biggest mistake of his life. He tapped the edge of his ticket against the palm of his hand, eyed the check-in counter, and weighed his options. One, he could fly home as planned and continue trying to make their relationship work through phone calls, letters, and now e-mail. But even the latest technology wasn't able to bridge a gap of two hundred miles and bring them together for a weekly game of Scrabble or a romantic dinner out. And even that wouldn't have been enough.

His other option was to stay in Rendezvous, rent a place in town, and propose. Selling his house had been on his mind for months, but he'd always stopped before taking the plunge and actually calling a Realtor. The more he thought about it, though, the house was far too big, too quiet. . .and Pricilla wasn't there.

There was another thing to consider as well. He'd been praying about his relationship with Pricilla for the past few days, and somehow he knew that if he walked away now, he'd lose her forever. How he'd allowed stubbornness and his own reservations to get him this far, he wasn't sure, but there was no way to get around the truth. He was lonely, and he loved her.

Not that he was looking simply for companionship. Not at all. Despite Pricilla's somewhat quirky ways at times and the fact that she seemed to have a nose for trouble, he still wanted her in his life—for the rest of his life. She made him smile like no one else could. She was funny, smart, and made his heart thud like he was seventeen again. He'd never win her heart completely if he didn't take a chance.

And this time his staying would have nothing to do with Reggie Pierce's death, or whether or not Annabelle was truly innocent. While it was true he worried about Pricilla's often unconventional attempts to play the role of amateur detective á la Jessica Fletcher, he couldn't change who she was. . .nor did he want to. It was part of what he loved about her. Her innate desire to find out the truth no matter how difficult the process.

The automatic doors opened beside him, allowing the scent of freshly mown grass to fill the air. He took in a deep breath and smiled in resolve. Just because they weren't in what society called the prime of their lives was no reason they couldn't find a bit of happiness together. Since living hundreds of miles apart wasn't working, it was time he stepped up and made the move. What difference did it really make anyway, whether he was in New Mexico or Colorado? Only one option would give him what he really wanted.

Grabbing his suitcase in one hand and his carry-on in the other, he stepped to the curb and flagged down a taxi.

Pricilla bent down and snipped off another daffodil to add to the bunch she already had in her hand. A fresh bouquet of flowers, even with her limited choices at this time of year, would go a long way to boost her spirits. She fingered the yellow bloom. With Max gone, she'd finally get a chance to be able to sort through her feelings. She needed the space to decide if she really was suffering from a case of cold feet. . .or if she was ready to take the plunge into something more permanent.

Like matrimony.

The word brought an assortment of feelings to the surface that only forty-three years married to the same man could bring. Like any couple, her and Marty's life together had been full of joy and disappointment, hard work and fun, struggles and contentment. Then life had intervened and taken Marty from her. His dying, while a part of life, had never been an easy phase for her. A time to be born and a time to die. A time to grieve and a time to dance. A time to love. . .

And for her a second chance for love?

Glancing up, she saw no signs, in the cloudless blue sky, of the plane that was taking Max back to New Mexico. All she could see were the Rocky Mountains that loomed between them. Perhaps the truth was that the distance between them had kept her from having to make a decision. But the time for decision was coming.

She walked slowly along the front of the lodge then stopped and clipped a few cuts of ferns for the bouquet. Beside her small herb garden, the grounds would soon be sprinkled with a covering of spring flowers. Bleeding hearts, sweet William, tiger lilies, and peonies. . . If her heavenly Creator cared about each colorful bloom, He certainly cared about her own personal dilemma. Glad that no one was around to hear her audible mumblings, she cut a sprig of rosemary for supper and began praying.

"The truth is, Lord, I am finally happy for the first time since Marty died. Nathan needs me here, and honestly, it's good to feel needed." She crumbled the blades of rosemary between her fingers and took in a deep breath of the fragrant herb.

Despite the hectic pace, she loved the chance to cook, create menus, and make the guests happy. Retirement, in her mind, had been as eventful as one of her prized cheese soufflés gone flat. Dull, dreary, and monotonous. No matter how strong her feelings were for Max, she needed a purpose for her life.

"What do you think, Lord? Maybe I'm just afraid I'll move to New Mexico only to have everything fall apart, leaving me with nothing."

It was better this way. Wasn't it?

A horn honked as a car pulled into the circular drive. Pricilla stood up and immediately regretted the abrupt move. "Who in the world. . . ?"

Rubbing the small of her back with her free hand, she squinted into the afternoon sun and tried to determine who was in the taxi. No new guests were scheduled to arrive until tomorrow, and rarely did anyone show up without a reservation, as the lodge stayed full most of the year.

The car stopped in front of the porch, and someone stepped out of the back seat. With his back toward her, the man set his suitcase and carry-on bag on the ground then turned to pay the driver.

Max? It couldn't be. He was twenty thousand feet up in the air. . . .

"Pricilla."

Leaving his bags beside the porch, Max walked toward her with a lopsided grin on his face. "I had this crazy idea about staying here in Colorado. Renting an apartment, taking you out to dinner once a week, maybe working part-time for your son as a handyman. I don't know. But what I do know is that it would beat long-distance phone calls and e-mails." He paused to take a breath. "What do you think?"

"I. . ." She pulled the flowers to her chest and felt her heart pounding against the crushed blooms. "I don't know what to say."

He stopped right in front of her. "Say that you want me to stay. That you wouldn't mind putting up with an old, retired, and rather predictable gentleman, who loves fishing, peach cobbler, and you, though certainly not in that order—"

She reached out and placed her finger against his lips, smiling at his nervous chatter. "I want you to stay."

"Really?" He grasped her hand. "Something told me that if I left today I'd lose you forever. I'm just not willing to do that."

"I don't want to lose you either." Pricilla shook her head, certain she was dreaming. He was really willing to give it all up for her? "What about your house, your hunting buddies. . .your life in New Mexico? You'd give it all up? For me?"

"Yes, because I'd like to give it. . .to give us. . .a try."

Pricilla's lips curled into a smile. She let the bouquet

of flowers tumble to the ground and wrapped her arms around his neck. Only God knew what the future held, but for the first time in a long while everything seemed all right again in the world.

Max looked across the table in the Rendezvous Bar and Grill, noted Pricilla's flushed cheeks, and knew he'd made the right decision. While she studied the dessert menu posted at the end of the table, he knew her mind wasn't on which piece of pie she might order but on their relationship. Not that Pricilla was ready to say yes to his proposal if he asked her today. He knew that. But he'd finally be able to court her properly. And what did he really have to lose? He could always fly back and go hunting with his buddies once or twice a year. And he'd be with Pricilla the rest of the time.

She sneezed and picked up her sweater off the bench beside her. Her notebook fell out on the table along with a packet of tissues.

Max reached across the table and picked up the spiral pad.

A grimace crossed her face as she grabbed it back. "You're not going to get after me for playing the role of Miss Marple again, are you?"

"No, because I know that if I do you'll have me running back to New Mexico faster than a wild bronco." He winked at her. He'd already decided that he was going to quit worrying about her investigative tendencies, even if that meant taking on the role of Dr.

Watson to her Sherlock Holmes.

"Good. Then I suppose I could keep you around."

Her laughter and smile made his pulse race. "Where are you in your questioning?"

Pricilla flipped open the notebook then set it in front of him. "I've gone through each of the suspects one by one, including, of course, the bakery's three full-time workers. Also on the list are Ezri and Stewart, and as much as I believe she's innocent, I couldn't completely eliminate Annabelle. I've also added Ezri's mystery man since he seems to always show up at interesting times and is somehow connected to her."

"What about outsiders?"

"While I realize that it's possible that someone outside this list was responsible for Reggie's demise, no one reported seeing anyone else on the premises that morning." For the first time since his return, she frowned. "Without the added benefit of the forensic science information the detective has, I've decided to keep my list to these seven. But as you can see, motivations are quite limited."

Max couldn't help but chuckle inside. He might have taught her a thing or two about the art of interrogation from his own experiences in the military, but it was obvious she was struggling this time around. On television the suspects often seem ready to confess at the end of the show, but in real life, he found that was rarely the case. That was certainly true right now.

The waitress brought two orders of French dip and salads, set them on the table in front of them, and promised to return with refills on their water. After asking the blessing for the meal, Max chomped into his sandwich, hungrier than he'd realized. Watching Pricilla eat, he realized how much he enjoyed moments like this. Moments together he'd like to get used to.

She reached out and grabbed Max's hand. She jutted her chin toward the counter. "It's him again."

Max leaned forward. "Who?"

"Ezri's mystery man. He's paying for an order of takeout." Pricilla scooted to the edge of the booth and squinted through the top of her bifocals. "He's not getting away from me this time."

8

Pricilla reached for her sweater, but Max stopped her by tightening his grip on her hand. "It's one thing to take a tour of the bakery and meet Annabelle's workers. But you don't know anything about this man. What if he's the murderer and you start asking him a bunch of pointed questions? What if. . ."

Max stopped and rubbed his temple with the finger-tips of his free hand. He'd practically accused a complete stranger of being involved in Reggie's death. For all he knew, the man could be a minister or a doctor. The whole situation was getting completely out of hand. Besides that, the young man was half his age and obviously worked out. No match for either of them if accusations began to fly and things got ugly. Dealing with this man would take a gun and a badge behind any finger pointing.

"I just want to talk to him." Pricilla pulled her hand away. "Annabelle is desperate for answers. If she goes to jail, what about her children and her business?"

He took in a deep breath and reminded himself of all the reasons why he'd decided to give up his life in New Mexico to spend it with Pricilla. "That's what I love about you. You've always cared about people enough to get involved in their lives. But this is different. Tell the sheriff about your suspicions and let him talk to the guy this time."

She shook her head. "All I'm going to do is ask him a few questions."

"Like what?" Max turned around to get a second glance at the man. "He's huge, and I don't think he's one to chat about a murder investigation over a cup of tea—especially if you're naming him as a suspect."

Pricilla's jaw tensed as she watched the front counter. The man was still waiting for his order. "All I plan to do is mention that I saw him with Ezri, and how I wondered if he was a friend of hers."

Leaning forward, Max lowered his voice. "And then what? Do you really think he's going to open up and tell you, a complete stranger, that he murdered Reggie? Or perhaps how he planned the man's demise with Ezri's help?"

"Max!"

"I'm sorry, but—"

"What about Sherlock Holmes and Dr. Watson?" Pricilla grabbed her notebook off the table. "I thought we were a team."

"We are, but—"

"He's just got his order. I've got to catch him before he gets away."

Before Max could mutter another word, she'd slid out of the booth and was gone. He eyed his sandwich and salad and felt his stomach growl. So much for lunch. With a resigned sigh, he headed for the front of the restaurant where Pricilla was leaving in pursuit of Ezri's mystery man, who carried a bag of takeout under his arm. Even Pricilla's suspect was going to get to eat lunch.

"Sir."

Max paused in the doorway at the cashier's sharp voice.

"Sir, you haven't paid."

Max turned around. Of all the ridiculous things. But he couldn't argue. The teenager, sporting a silver nose ring and eying him accusingly, was right. Pricilla was going to get him into serious trouble one day. He could see the headlines now: MAN ARRESTED FOR FAILING TO PAY FOR LUNCH. He took a deep breath and dug his wallet out of his pocket. Twenty dollars would more than cover the bill and leave a hefty tip to a waitress who had yet to refill their water. He set the money on the counter.

She chomped on a piece of gum and glared at him. "I need to see your bill with that."

"I don't have a bill."

"Then you'll have to wait until the waitress rings one up for you."

This conversation was going nowhere quickly. "I'm in a hurry, can't you—"

"I need the bill."

Max scanned the crowded restaurant for the waitress, but there was no sign of the redhead. "You can still see what I ordered on my table, because I didn't have a chance to finish it. Two orders of French dip sandwiches and salads. Water to drink. Nothing on your menu is over nine bucks."

The girl was still frowning.

Max slapped another five on the counter. "Will this cover any inconvenience?"

She fingered the additional bill. "Well, I suppose this would cover whatever was on the bill—"

"Thank you." Max hurried out the door and glanced

up and down Main Street for Pricilla's bright pink sweater.

She was nowhere to be seen.

⌁

Pricilla slipped around the corner of Main and Aspen and pressed her hand against her chest. Max had been wrong. Ezri's mystery man's physique wasn't proving to be a physical threat to her life, but his fast pace might. The man was only half a block ahead of her, but so far he hadn't heard her attempts to get his attention. More than likely he was listening to one of those new-fangled headsets with music loud enough to leave him deaf before he was thirty.

Trying to control her labored breathing, she walked past the local pet shop and wished she'd worn her walking shoes. If he went much farther, she'd have to admit defeat. He had to be stopping soon, though. The only thing left on this street was the snowmobile shop on the corner. Beyond that, the paved road turned into a dirt path that led up into the mountains.

A large neon sign stood in front of the one-story building that rented snowmobiles and ATVs to tourists. Pricilla's eyes widened as the man struck off across the parking lot where a couple dozen all-terrain vehicles were parked.

"Surely he's not planning to ride one of those. . ."

The man jumped on one of the ATVs.

Pricilla shook her head and scurried toward him, but he was too far away. She'd never reach him in time. "No, no, no. . ."

Quickly she weighed her options. There wasn't a salesperson in sight to help her. Not that they would want to rent to a gray-haired granny sporting heels and a pleated skirt. He gunned the engine. Pricilla waved her arms to get his attention, but he was busy getting his helmet on.

She eyed one of the models. The key was in the ignition. Once, about fifteen years ago, she and Marty had rented a couple of ATVs and ridden for several hours through the desert. Maneuvering an ATV might not be like driving a car, but how hard could it be? The man was pulling out of the parking lot. She couldn't simply take it, of course. And besides, she wasn't even sure she could remember how to start the thing.

"You've done this before, and it can't be that difficult." Pricilla hiked her leg over the seat and tried turning the key.

Nothing.

She had to hurry. She could still see the flame-colored vehicle as the man headed down the dirt trail, but it wouldn't be long until he disappeared from view behind the trees. She tried turning the key again and this time the engine roared to life. There was a helmet on the handlebars, and she shoved it on her head before buckling the strap.

No doubt this was one of those situations where Max would demand she stop and consider carefully what she was about to do. But a picture of Annabelle flashed through her mind. She'd mentioned her fears that Ezri was seeing someone and had been very secretive about the relationship. Pricilla had seen firsthand how one bad egg could ruin a girl for life. Maybe there was no connection to Reggie's death, but she'd never forgive herself if she didn't at least try.

The vehicle jerked forward, almost knocking her off. She was going to get herself killed before ever leaving the parking lot. Inching forward, she pushed harder on the accelerator, allowing it to sputter ahead. One hand on the gas, the other on the brake, it was simple. All she had to do was follow Ezri's mystery man and find out where he was staying. With an extra spurt of gas to the engine, she flew forward toward the dirt road.

9

Max stood on the edge of the sidewalk, wondering how Pricilla could have simply vanished. Her car was still parked in front of the Rendezvous Bar and Grill, which meant she couldn't have gone far, but a glance down both sides of the street revealed nothing more than a couple small groups of tourists enjoying a day of shopping. Which way had she gone?

Frustrated, he headed north on Main, glancing into store windows in hopes of catching a glimpse of her pink sweater behind a display of old-fashioned trunks or maybe a rack of postcards. Three blocks later, he paused again at the corner boasting the only stoplight in town. Considering the town of Rendezvous had only one main street, there weren't a lot of places where one could simply disappear. Straight ahead led to the park. To the right was the road to Nathan's lodge, and the road to the left went past an ATV rental place as it began its ascent into the mountains. He simply had no idea which way to go.

Knowing Pricilla's inclination to get into trouble didn't help calm his anxiety either. He scratched behind his ear and decided to backtrack along the other side of the street. There had to be a logical explanation somewhere. If Pricilla's mystery man was connected to Ezri, it made sense that Pricilla had followed him back to the bakery. If nothing else, it was worth a try.

Crossing the street, he admitted to himself that

his decision to return to Rendezvous was not turning out the way he'd expected. In less than an hour, he'd assumed his role of Dr. Watson despite his better judgment, paid for a supposed celebratory meal he hadn't had a chance to enjoy, and lost Pricilla. How could the woman be such a magnet for trouble?

As Max approached the bakery, a flash of color caught his eye at the end of the alley that ran alongside the store. He adjusted his bifocals. It was definitely not Pricilla, but someone was rummaging through a bag beside a Dumpster. He took a couple steps into the alley. It was Naldo—or José. He couldn't tell for sure which brother, but there was one thing he could tell. The man wasn't taking out the trash. Max watched as the other man pulled out a dark green sack from the large Dumpster and began sifting through its contents. Every few seconds he glanced back at the bakery, then continued his search.

Max searched for a legitimate explanation. Not that going through trash was unheard of. He knew about the sport of Dumpster diving from a nephew of his who claimed he'd given up shopping retail because of his regular dives. But except for a few stale donuts and bagels, Max couldn't imagine what one of the Baker's Dozen employees would be doing sorting through trash. And considering that the bakery was the site of a recent murder, he couldn't help but wonder if there was a connection.

He strolled past the alley, trying to look inconspicuous by appearing to be interested in the latest spring collection of women's wear displayed in a store window. He counted to thirty, then spun around to return for a second look down the alley. The man was gone. Max didn't stop to consider the consequences. He slipped down the alley and found the grocery sack the man had been going through. It was nothing more than a bunch of discarded mail, mainly junk mail, the kind that had a habit of collecting faster than the layer of dust in his living room.

He picked up one of the envelopes from the sack, flipped it over, and read the address. Darren Robinson. He picked up another envelope from a credit card company. Again, the letter had been forwarded to the bakery and addressed to Darren Robinson.

A door squeaked open behind him. Max shoved a piece of the mail into his back pocket, threw the rest of the evidence into the Dumpster, and spun around.

Annabelle stood in the doorway, dressed in a blue jogging suit. "Why, Mr. Summers. What a surprise. It's good to see you again."

"I'm afraid I've. . ." He stammered, irritated that he'd let his curiosity get the best of him. And he'd gotten onto Pricilla for being impulsive.

"Did you need something?" The smile on the woman's lips didn't mask the dark shadows under her eyes.

"I'm looking for Pricilla, actually. Have you seen her?"

"Not today." If the women found it odd that she'd caught him behind her shop, going through the Dumpster, she didn't show it.

"I'm sure she's fine, she. . ." He didn't know how to explain the fact that he'd managed to lose Pricilla while eating lunch in town.

"You know, your timing is perfect, if you have a few minutes."

"My timing?"

"Ezri's out, Stewart's working up front, and Naldo just finished baking a new batch of samples. We need someone to taste them."

Max took in a deep breath of chocolate, caramel, and every other sinfully delicious pastry the bakery made and wondered how he could refuse. "But Pricilla. . ."

"I can have Stewart send her back if she shows up." She waved him inside. "Do you like macaroons?"

He followed her to a table set up on the far side of the room. "If you're talking about one of those divine coconut cookies Pricilla likes to make for her guests."

"That's exactly what I'm talking about, but these are homemade coconut almond macaroons filled with bittersweet chocolate cream and just a hint of orange marmalade inside."

Max's mouth began to water.

"Don't forget the bittersweet chocolate and roasted coconut on the outside."

He smiled. "And you want me to be a taste tester."

"Are you game?"

He glanced at the door. "I really should try and find Pricilla. . ."

"It will take five minutes, and I'm sure she's fine. Mr. Cadwell is having a shoe sale. Fifty percent off. She told me she planned to stop by and probably just forgot to tell you."

Max hesitated. Annabelle was right. Letting his

imagination get away from him was only going to up his blood pressure. He worried too much. Just because Reggie Pierce had met a tragic ending didn't mean there was a murderer around every corner. Besides that, he knew how much Pricilla loved to talk. He eyed the tray of desserts and cleared his throat. Pricilla was fine.

"I don't ever remember turning down a chance to sample desserts of any kind. Especially when the words *chocolate*, *coconut*, and *orange marmalade* are all in the same sentence."

"And that's not all," Annabelle rushed on. "We're trying out a new triple chocolate cheesecake, and raspberry bars—raspberry preserves inside a buttery, almond crumb crust."

Max rested a hand on his stomach, knowing exactly what Pricilla would say if she were here. But surely calories didn't matter for the moment. Naldo and José were busy at work. He could always use the opportunity to see if what had just happened outside at the Dumpster had any relevance to the case.

"You're going to love these." Annabelle sat down at a small table and motioned for Max to join her. "Naldo wants to add a few more choices to our selection and prepared these to see what I think."

"I saw Naldo, or maybe his brother, outside a couple of minutes ago."

"Naldo stepped out for a bit of air, I believe. Are you ready?"

He eyed a tray filled with samples of dessert and smiled. A few minutes longer wouldn't hurt. Annabelle picked up a bite-sized macaroon and Max followed suit.

The creamy chocolate blending in with the coconut and marmalade swirled on his taste buds.

"Now this is fantastic."

"I agree, but there's more."

Max took a second bite of the macaroon for good measure, certain that moving to Rendezvous was going to prove to be hazardous to his health. Between the bakery and Pricilla's cooking he wasn't sure how he was going to avoid gaining weight.

He took a sip of water from the glass Annabelle offered then eyed the next selection. Cheesecake was one of his favorites. A buzzer went off across the kitchen and Max glanced up. Naldo and José, along with a couple helpers, were hard at work baking. Now was as good a time as any to voice his recent concerns.

"I know it's none of my business," he began, "but Naldo was sifting through the trash in your Dumpster."

Annabelle looked up. "That's odd."

"I thought so as well, though normally I suppose I wouldn't feel compelled to say anything. It's just that with the death of your husband. . ." He caught her flickering gaze. "I'm sorry."

"It's okay. I appreciate your concern." She picked up a bite-sized piece of cheesecake. "While I can't imagine why he would go through the Dumpster, I also don't see how it could have any connection to my husband's death."

"Normally I would agree. What struck me, though, was that he was looking through Darren Robinson's mail."

"That's even stranger." She wiped the corners of her mouth with a napkin. "But I still can't see a connection to my husband's death. Can you?"

"No. . . Not at the moment anyway."

Max pulled out the envelope from his back pocket. It had been forwarded, in care of the bakery. "Does Darren have all his mail forwarded here?"

"Yes. He said it would be easier for him since he was only going to be here temporarily and doesn't have a permanent address."

Max set the letter on the table and reached for a raspberry bar. "Where is he living right now?"

"He moved in with a couple friends on the edge of town. I don't think it's anything worth bragging about, but the rent is cheap and the neighborhood is decent."

He took a bite of the crunchy raspberry bar and smiled. At least this wasn't a competition. He'd never be able to choose his favorite of the three.

Annabelle took a sip of her water. "I could simply ask Naldo what he was doing."

"I'm not sure that's a good idea. I think it best to leave all lines of questioning to the police—"

"Naldo."

His concern fell on deaf ears. So much for trying not to get involved. How was he ever going to convince Pricilla about the dangers of investigating once she knew what he'd been up to?

Naldo stopped at the table with a broad smile across his face. He wiped his hands against his white apron that was covered with flour and smears of chocolate.

"Mrs. Pierce? Do you like them?"

"You've outdone yourself again, Naldo. As always."

"Mr. . . ."

Max nodded. "Mr. Summers. Max Summers."

"Do you like them, Mr. Summers?"

"They're fantastic."

Naldo moved to leave, but Annabelle stopped him. "There is one other small thing, Naldo. I'm sure it's nothing, but with the recent death of my husband, you must understand that I'm. . .concerned about what happens around here."

Naldo's brow lowered. "Of course, Mrs. Pierce."

Annabelle picked up the envelope from the table and handed it to Naldo. "Mr. Summers, as a friend, is looking into the death of my husband and saw you going through the trash. Looking specifically, it seems, in Darren Robinson's mail. I wondered if you could tell me why."

"I. . ." Naldo glanced away briefly. "I received a letter from home this week and can't find it. I thought perhaps it had gotten thrown away with the trash. I have no reason to look through Darren's mail."

Max was certain the man was lying.

"You know that Mr. Pierce always treated my brother and me well," Naldo continued. "I never would have done anything to hurt him. . .or you and his children."

"I know that, Naldo. Thank you for your explanation. You and your brother have always been hard workers and you know I appreciate that. I was certain you had a plausible explanation."

"Thank you, ma'am." Naldo bowed his head then returned to the kitchen.

"You don't believe him, do you?" A shadow crossed Annabelle's face as she picked up another raspberry bar and took a bite.

"I believe he respects you and your late husband, though I'm not convinced about his excuse. But you were right. It's probably nothing." Max looked at his watch. "I really should go and find Pricilla."

"Of course." Annabelle stood. "Thank you for your help with the pastries. . .and for your concern for me and my family."

Max said good-bye then hurried out the back alley to the street. Just like he'd done with Pricilla's disappearance, he refused to make a mountain out of a molehill, but one thing seemed obvious. Naldo was hiding something.

Every joint of Pricilla's body ached from the continual jolt of the uneven terrain as she rode the ATV up the bumpy mountain road. She already regretted her impulsive decision and knew she should stop. The only problem was that she wasn't sure if she could stop. And of course, at some point she'd return the quad. She'd simply have to explain that she'd been after a suspect in a murder investigation, and if she lost the man she might miss an important lead. She'd worry then whether or not they believed her.

Another bump on the road shook the ATV. Not

only were the trees lining the trail getting denser, but the dirt road was getting steeper, and she wasn't sure anymore that the owners of the ATV she'd "borrowed" were going to look at her acquisition that way. Why couldn't she have simply admitted defeat and waited for a more opportune time to track down the man?

Except who was to say that she'd ever get another chance. Keeping her speed constant, she somehow managed to keep the other vehicle in sight. The driver had made no sign that he noticed anyone was behind him, which was fine with her. She'd much rather keep her presence undisclosed than have him think someone was stalking him.

A large bump in the road bounced her ATV into the air. Slamming down on the seat, she realized the truth in the saying that you're only as young as you feel, because at the moment, she was feeling quite old. Her body, with all the normal aches and pains of a sixty-five-year-old, wasn't meant to fly down a dirt road—in a skirt, no less—on an off-road vehicle.

She gripped the handles and attempted to avoid a second bump, but that only managed to pull her off course. The ATV veered off the path and she lost control. A tree loomed ahead of her. Pulling to the right with every ounce of strength she had left, she missed the tree by inches. . .and ran into a juniper shrub. Entangled by the bush, the engine sputtered then stopped.

With her entire body numb from the vibration of the vehicle, Pricilla didn't move for a full thirty seconds. Finally, she pulled the helmet off her head and assessed the damages. Her skirt had caught on something and was torn. A bruise was forming on her left calf, and her arms felt like limp spaghetti. At least she'd live.

Pricilla drew in a sharp breath and tried to ignore the stab of pain in her lungs, brought on by the cool mountain air. A lark called out in the distance. Blue spruce, evergreens, and aspen trees crowded around her. A crisp, spring wind blew across her face, but all she felt was a deep ache in every muscle and joint. Climbing slowly off the bike, she stood up straight. She'd be sore tomorrow—and the day after that, no doubt. What she really wanted right now was a hot bath with a handful of Epsom salts thrown in. Instead, she had two options, and they both, unfortunately, involved exercise. Walk back to town, or continue on to the nearest cabin. She adjusted her bifocals and looked ahead. There was a cabin not five hundred yards from her. . .with the flame-colored ATV parked outside.

Leaving the quad bike to be dealt with later, Pricilla made her way toward the cabin, stopping only once she'd reached the bottom of the porch stairs. The one-story house sat surrounded by a grove of aspen trees, and a trail of smoke rose from the chimney. But there was no trace of the man. Max was going to be furious at her impulsiveness, but she'd come this far. She might as well go the rest of the way.

With a dose of determination, she marched up the steps and knocked on the door. Someone pulled back a lace curtain and peered out the front window. A moment later the door opened.

"Mrs. Crumb?"

"Ezri?" Pricilla wasn't sure who was the most surprised.

Ezri tugged on the bottom of her tan leather jacket and cocked her head. "Mrs. Crumb? I—"

"Who is it, sweetheart?" Ezri's mystery man stepped in behind her and peered over her head.

Priscilla cleared her throat. "This is rather awkward, and I am sorry for barging in on you like this, Ezri, as it's really none of my business, but. . .you know, I haven't met your friend."

"This is Kent Walters." Ezri glanced behind her. "My. . .my husband."

Your husband? Oh." Pricilla's eyes widened as she tried to process Ezri's statement. "I had no idea you were married."

"Neither did anyone else until now." Kent, who towered over Ezri by several inches, came forward and shook Pricilla's hand. "It's nice to meet you, Mrs. Crumb."

Ezri ignored her husband's questioning stare. "Mrs. Crumb, you must be cold. Please come in."

Pricilla shivered in response. "I'm fine, really, though it is a bit chilly now that the sun has started going down."

"You can sit by the fire and warm up." Ezri pulled a stack of books off a worn wingback chair and patted the back of the seat. "Would you like some hot chocolate? I've even got some of those miniature marshmallows."

"That would be nice. Thank you." Pricilla went to stand in front of the hearth, not sure if the chills she felt were from the weather or the strange situation she'd just stepped into.

The fire crackled, and she breathed in the fresh scent of pine. Pricilla fingered the notebook inside her skirt pocket and mentally added two questions to her list. Was there any connection in all of this to Reggie's death? Or had she simply uncovered a whole other mystery? Somehow, she knew she needed to find out the answers to both, because whether or not Ezri had been involved with her father's death, Pricilla had obviously stumbled onto something significant.

Ezri hesitated for a moment in the doorway to the kitchen as if she wasn't quite sure whether or not Pricilla should be left alone with Kent. "I'll be right back with the hot chocolate."

Pricilla's adrenaline raced as she glanced around the room. The small living area was sparsely furnished, but red fringed throw pillows, paired with a multicolored afghan on the couch and a handful of pictures, added just enough warmth to make the room homey. While she was shocked to hear that Ezri was married—a fact she was quite certain her mother had no inkling of—at least a cup of hot chocolate might give her time to figure out exactly what was going on.

Pricilla's gaze stopped at a wedding photo of Ezri and Kent. Unlike the trendy jacket, T-shirt, and low-cut jeans Ezri wore today, the white dress was simple and elegant.

She picked up the silver frame off the mantel to study the picture closer. "Ezri made a beautiful bride."

Kent cleared his throat. "Yes, she did."

He turned to her, allowing Pricilla to get a close look at him for the first time. Standing at least six foot two, he was muscular with bright blue eyes, and quite handsome. His expression softened as he gazed at the photo of his wife. While Max had to be correct in his assessment that the man worked out, there was nothing sinister about him. Just from the look in his eyes, it was obvious that he loved Ezri.

Pricilla ran her finger down the edge of the frame.

"It's too bad her mother wasn't able to help plan the wedding."

"I guess you've figured out by now that we married in a very untraditional manner." He picked up a piece of candy out of a bowl from the hearth and unwrapped it. "I tried to talk her out of eloping, but Ezri insisted we keep it a secret."

Pricilla set the photo back down and took a seat in the wingback chair. "Why the secrecy?"

"You'll have to ask Ezri that question." He popped the chocolate into his mouth. "I'm not even sure why she told you who I was. She's the one who insisted that we keep our relationship a secret. Something hard to do as a newlywed, let me tell you."

Pricilla caught his slight blush. "How long have you been married?"

"Almost two months." He shoved the wrapper into his jeans pocket and reached for a second piece of candy. "I've seen you around town, haven't I?"

"Perhaps." Pricilla nodded, wondering how much she should admit to regarding her afternoon escapade. "I. . .I have to confess that I followed you here today."

She braced for his response, hoping she wouldn't be the only one coming clean.

"You followed me here?"

"I borrowed one of the ATVs from town." Pricilla cringed, realizing how lame her excuse was going to sound. The way things were headed, she'd be the one ending up in a jail cell.

"Really? I'm working at the shop for the summer. They let me use one of their ATVs to get around.

Renting a car became too expensive." He shook his head. "I don't understand, though. Why were you following me?"

Ezri returned with two large mugs of hot chocolate and handed one to Pricilla. "Kent, please. Mrs. Crumb is a close friend of my mother's. I'm sure she has a perfectly good reason. Don't you, Mrs. Crumb?"

"Ezri, can I talk to you in the kitchen for a minute?" He turned to Pricilla, his expression guarded. "You don't mind, do you, Mrs. Crumb?"

"Kent—"

"I don't mind at all." Pricilla touched the young woman's sleeve. "Really, Ezri, it's fine. And by the time you get back, I might actually have warmed up enough to chat for a few minutes."

Pricilla took a sip of the chocolate and let the hot liquid warm her insides as the couple left the room. Not that Ezri would want to chat with her. Pricilla had somehow managed to show up unannounced on their doorstep and gain a confession before she'd even posed her first question. She bet the detective couldn't have done that well if he'd tried. But that still left her with the fact that Ezri was feeling vulnerable, and answering a slew of questions might not go over well.

Two minutes later the back door slammed shut as Ezri returned to the living room again. "You'll have to forgive Kent. He knows how badly I've been hurt in the past with my father, and he's always been very protective of me. He wasn't sure how to react with your showing up unexpectedly and then my blurting out that we're married."

"He seems like a nice man." Pricilla prayed for wisdom as she spoke. Outside appearances often meant nothing. A secret marriage could easily be the tip of the iceberg for a multitude of other skeletons. And she couldn't forget Reggie's murder.

"Kent is wonderful." Ezri sat on the edge of the brick hearth with a dreamy look of one in love. "He spoils me like I'm a princess."

For a moment, Pricilla saw the familiar reflection of her own self all those years ago. She, too, had been young, in love, and ready to conquer the world with her hero. Losing Marty had been like losing half of her soul. And it had taught her that happily ever after doesn't last forever.

Starting a relationship with Max had been completely unexpected. He'd waltzed into her life like a handsome knight on horseback and reminded her of the delights of falling in love for the first time. Having cold feet hadn't stopped her heart from beating fast in his presence or her cheeks from blushing at his compliments. Somehow, Max had managed to start erasing any doubts she harbored over finding love the second time.

But she wasn't here for Max.

Pushing thoughts of her own romantic saga aside, Pricilla pressed on with the matter at hand. "Tell me about Kent."

Ezri stretched out her legs and crossed her ankles. "I met him two years ago in an English lit class. For me, it was love at first sight. He was so handsome and dreamy, like Jane Austen's Mr. Darcy and Lord Byron wrapped up into one."

Pricilla laughed at the comparison. "As I recall from my own literature classes, Lord Byron was somewhat of a scandalous hero, was he not?"

Ezri leaned forward and winked. "Eloping is rather scandalous, don't you think?"

"True." If thoughts of scandal hadn't stopped Ezri from going ahead with the elopement, Pricilla couldn't help but wonder what else the young woman might dare to try. Murder, perhaps? "Kent seemed surprised that you told me the truth about your marriage. And, I have to admit, so was I."

Ezri shrugged. "Even I'm astounded over the confession. I don't know. I saw you standing there with Kent behind me, and it just slipped out. Truth is, I'm tired of keeping secrets and sneaking around. It's been awful not telling my mother."

Pricilla shook her head. She had yet to understand the couple's reasoning for keeping the relationship a secret. "If it's been so awful, then why haven't you told her?"

Ezri took a sip of her drink then held the steamy cup under her chin. "It's complicated."

"Love often is, but I'd think your mother would be thrilled to know that you've found someone who loves you so much."

"I know." Ezri's relaxed pose was fading. "I used to have dreams of a beautiful church wedding, with me in a long satin dress with a train that went on forever. Funny how life sometimes gets in the way."

"What exactly got in the way?"

"You mean who." Ezri fiddled with the gold chain

of her necklace. "It was my father. While everyone knew he could be temperamental, I'm sure my mother kept certain things even from you. He was extremely controlling. For example, in order to pay for our schooling, we had to return home every summer and work at the bakery where he paid us minimum wage and made us miserable. Marriage was another issue with him. Not that he was against my getting married one day, I suppose, but not until I had a diploma in my hand. If he knew I'd married Kent, he'd have cut me off financially, and then I wouldn't have been able to afford to stay in school."

Pricilla didn't like where the conversation was heading. "So this is all about money?"

Ezri frowned. "You make me sound like a fortune hunter."

"But why not just wait?"

Ezri took a sip of her hot chocolate and spilled a drop on her shirt. She pulled a tissue out of her pocket and dabbed at the stain. "Kent wouldn't have waited for me forever."

"If he truly loves you—"

"Please, Mrs. Crumb." Ezri set her mug on the hearth and walked across the worn carpet. "I know enough to realize that no guy is going to wait around for a girl whose father dominates her life and refuses to let her marry."

Pricilla understood the girl's dilemma but still wasn't convinced that Kent had been worth the deception. "What about the fight you had with Kent after your father's funeral? I hate to say it, but from what I saw, he seemed as domineering as your father."

"Kent is nothing like my father." Ezri stopped in front of the fireplace and faced Pricilla. "He's kind, gentle, compassionate. . . ." She shook her head and threw the tissue into the fire. Within seconds it had disintegrated. "He believed we should tell my mother that we're married, but I felt like she'd had enough shocking news lately."

"Your mother's stronger than you think, Ezri."

"Maybe, but losing a husband then finding out her daughter had eloped all in the same week didn't seem right." Ezri shrugged. "I guess I'm still waiting for the right moment."

"So Kent is living here while you wait to tell your mom?"

"This place belongs to his grandfather." Ezri ran her fingers across the stone hearth. "I love it up here on the mountain. And best of all, it gives us a place to be together when I'm not working at the bakery."

As a mother, Pricilla knew that if Ezri were her child, she'd want to know the truth. "You need to tell your mom."

"I know. But now she's dealing with my father's death, and the detective—"

"Keeping secrets only causes trouble in the end."

"Like murder?" Ezri sat back down. "Kent's one of your suspects, isn't he?"

"I'm not a detective."

"Mom told me that you were looking into things for her and trying to find out the truth. I guess Kent might have looked a bit suspicious if you didn't know who he was. Of course, I suppose I'm on the list as well, aren't I?"

Pricilla pressed her hand against her pocket and felt the notebook. "I admit to being curious. That's the reason I followed him here. I was worried about you."

Pricilla set her empty mug on the hearth and realized she was still just as worried about Ezri. With her father out of the picture, she could bring her marriage out into the open. Was freedom from her father motive enough for murder?

Ezri glanced outside where Kent was chopping wood. "So what now?"

"I'd say that's up to you."

※

When the neon sign of the snowmobile shop came into view, Pricilla felt her breath catch. She'd hardly noticed the bumps and ruts she'd traveled over for the past few minutes. All she'd been able to think about was Ezri's foolish elopement and her own foolish, impulsive act. While she'd tried to convince Ezri that it was time to face the truth and confess to her mother, she knew she had her own confession to make. Hopefully the owners of the four-wheeler would be sympathetic and not press charges.

Kent had offered to follow her back down to the shop and explain the situation to his boss, but Pricilla had graciously declined his offer, insisting that she was going to have to own up to her actions.

Pulling into the parking lot, she maneuvered past

a row of discounted bikes. Max had probably called the sheriff by now and put out a missing persons report on her. What was he going to say when he found out where she'd really been? She pressed on the brake and managed to stop without running into anything.

"There she is, Detective." A balding man came storming out of the shop with none other than Detective Carter on his tail. "I'd say the description I gave you fit perfectly. Late sixties, gray hair. . ."

Late sixties? Pricilla let out a sharp huff. That boy needed a new pair of glasses. Ignoring the commotion as the two men shuffled across the parking lot to where she had parked, she attempted to climb off the bike. Her legs went limp, and this time it wasn't from the jostling of the quad. Somehow she knew that whatever excuse she gave for her impulsive behavior, it wasn't going to work with the detective.

Gripping the handles, she braced herself for the encounter. "Detective Carter. I hadn't expected to run into you today."

"So you didn't plan to steal this quad bike?"

"I didn't steal it, I just. . ." Just what? For the first time in her life her curiosity and impulsiveness were about to give her a federal record. "I take full responsibility for my actions."

The detective shook his head. "Pricilla Crumb, I'm afraid I'm going to have to place you under arrest for the unauthorized possession of this all-terrain vehicle."

Pricilla clenched the arms of the metal chair in Detective Carter's small office and tried not to panic. Max had warned her that her attempts to play detective would only get her into trouble. And his predictions had just come true. The detective might not have forced her to wear handcuffs on the short ride to the sheriff's office, but she knew he was on his way to start the fingerprinting process followed by half a dozen mug shots. She glanced down at her black skirt and wondered what she'd look like in bright orange. Mouthwatering gourmet meals and walks in the mountains would be replaced by an hour of fresh air a day and manual labor.

Surely this wasn't happening.

Needing to focus on something besides her current state as an apprehended felon, she glanced around the office. Two glass walls overlooked the lobby of the station that was quiet at the moment. Obviously, no one else had decided to go chasing after a murder suspect in a pilfered off-road vehicle. The second pair of walls was lined with plaques and diplomas. It seemed the detective was creating a name for himself in the area of law enforcement.

Or at least trying to. Considering his brusque manners and gruff behavior, she still wasn't convinced of his competence.

Standing to examine the plaques more carefully,

she dismissed the thought and wondered why Detective Carter always managed to rub her the wrong way. He was just a man doing his best to get ahead in this world. And besides that, it couldn't be easy trying to live up to a reputation like his uncle's. Sheriff Tucker had spent seventeen years as a top-ranking officer in the New York police department before taking on a more quiet position as sheriff in the mountainous town of Rendezvous.

A photo of a woman and child sat on Carter's desk. Funny. She'd never thought of the detective as a family man. Because he'd always come across as cold, she'd always assumed he was single. Maybe those were qualities he left behind at the office.

Pricilla turned around as the glass door clicked open. "Detective, I was just looking at your photo. Is this your family?"

Carter set a folder on his desk. "My wife and daughter."

"Your wife is gorgeous, and so is your little girl. How old is she?"

"Sammy will be three next month."

Pricilla pointed to the displayed awards, hoping to avoid the inevitable booking procedure. "Quite impressive. Degrees in criminal justice and law couldn't have been easy."

The detective sat down at his desk with a shrug. "After a couple more years of experience under my belt, I'm planning on joining the FBI."

"That's a noble goal."

"One I've had since I was thirteen years old." He

picked up a pencil and tapped it against his desk. "Mrs. Crumb, enough of my life. I have some news you're going to be happy about."

She perched on the edge of her chair, wondering why his expression didn't match his words. "I could use some good news right now."

"The owners of the shop dropped the charges against you."

"Really?" A ripple of relief surged through her. "Why?"

"Kent managed to explain to them the reasoning behind the escapade. One that I have to admit I'm not quite clear on myself at this point. Chasing suspects and stealing vehicles are bound to get you in trouble."

She ignored the implications as she rose from her chair. "So I'm free to go?"

"Not quite yet." The man had yet to smile. "Have a seat, please."

"All right." She drew out her words, feeling as if she wasn't going to like where this conversation was headed.

The detective steepled his hands in front of him. "Mrs. Crumb, let's be honest for a few minutes. I know you don't like me."

A whoosh of air escaped her lungs. This was what he wanted to talk about? The constant clashing of their personalities? "Of course I don't dislike you, I just—"

"I said let's be honest, Mrs. Crumb." He held up his hand to stop her. "You dislike my straightforward methods to find justice. And most importantly, you dislike the fact that I'm about to arrest your friend for murder."

The mention of Annabelle soured her stomach. "Like you, all I want is for justice to be done, but Annabelle is innocent."

Carter shook his head. "That's not what the evidence says, but regardless of the facts of the case, let me try and put things a different way. I admire your deep passion to help people, but—"

"Really?" She ignored the *but*, finding it hard to believe that he admired anything about her, considering the mess she'd just gotten herself into.

"Yes, I do. But it's time that you and I came to an understanding. I'm the detective here, sworn to uphold the law. You, on the other hand, cook at a local lodge."

"I'm the chef—"

"Fine, so you're a chef at a local lodge. I thought I made myself clear during Charles Woodruff's murder investigation. You have no business following suspects, interrogating—"

"I never interrogated anyone." Her fleeting attempts to defend herself were likely to get her into more trouble, but there was no one else in the room to speak on her behalf. Perhaps she should have agreed to the offer for a lawyer after all. "Detective Carter, all I did was ask a few simple questions—"

"Please, Mrs. Crumb." He scratched the top of his bald head. "This isn't television where you snoop around until the murderer confesses his—or her—deadly deed. There's no prewritten script here. A man's been murdered and there's a killer on the loose. Neither is it a tea party or a Saturday morning with the knitting club."

Pricilla frowned. Just because she was old enough to be his grandmother didn't mean he had to stick her in the corner with a pair of knitting needles.

The detective leaned forward and caught her gaze. "What's it going to take to get you to leave things up to me?"

"Are you wanting to strike a deal?"

"No, I'm *wanting* you to stay out of my investigation."

Pricilla folded her arms across her chest. "Did you know that Kent and Ezri are married?"

Detective Carter shook his head. "I'm not following."

"It's just a simple question. Did you know that Kent Walters and Ezri Pierce are married?"

"No." He flipped his pencil against the desk. "Did you know that Stewart dropped out of school two months ago?"

Pricilla lowered her head. "No."

"What is your point then, Mrs. Crumb?" The detective leaned forward. "As you can see, you're not the only one capable of gathering pertinent information."

"I still believe that people will tell me things they would never tell you. And no matter what the evidence shows at this point, I'm acquainted with Annabelle well enough to know that she never would have killed her husband. There's a piece of the puzzle that is still missing."

"I'm afraid you're quite naïve, Mrs. Crumb. Refreshing, perhaps, to see in a person, but in the real world, it just doesn't work. How well do we really know anyone? I could quote case after case where the nice man next door was eventually arrested for some ghastly crime no one thought he could have committed."

"That's quite a cynical view of life, don't you think?"

"No, it's realistic. And the other thing to consider is that you don't hold a badge."

She knew he was right, but she couldn't forget the broken expression on Annabelle's face. There had to be something she could do. "So, what if I promise not to actively seek out new information regarding the investigation?"

Carter's forehead wrinkled into half a dozen narrow folds. "What does that mean?"

"It means that I won't chase after possible suspects on borrowed quad bikes—"

"*Stolen* quad bikes."

Pricilla tried not to choke on her next word. "Agreed."

"Here's the deal. If you happen to come across information regarding the death of Reggie Pierce, you may ask a few subtle questions, but you also will promise to pass on any information you receive directly to me."

Pricilla smiled. "So, I'm your. . .assistant."

"Absolutely not." Carter's expression morphed into one of disbelief. "But I can't forbid you from keeping your eyes and ears open. You'll pass on any information, and you'll avoid situations that get you arrested. Next time things might not go so easy for you on this end of the law."

"So, if I'm not your assistant, how about your stool pigeon?"

"My what?"

"Your mole." She couldn't help but beam as the detective squirmed in his seat. "You know. Your informant. Isn't that police lingo?"

A vein protruded in the detective's thick neck. "Mrs. Crumb, you are not working for me. You are not my informant or my mole. Do I make myself clear?"

"Perfectly."

"Good. Now you can go."

Pricilla leaned forward. "One last question. Do you happen to know where Max is? I thought he might have been worried and called here to find out where I was."

The detective jutted his chin toward the glass wall. Max was talking to the receptionist at the front desk. Her confidence vanished, leaving her feeling like a schoolgirl being picked up from the principal's office for unruly behavior.

Pricilla stood to thank the detective. In her quest for justice, she'd made a crucial mistake in disregarding the consequences. And Max was sure to be upset at her impulsiveness. It was time to see just what her actions were going to cost her.

～

Max barely had a chance to ask the receptionist about Pricilla's whereabouts before she emerged from the detective's office. After wandering around town another thirty minutes, asking shopkeepers if they'd seen her, he'd decided that his only alternative was to go to the sheriff.

He stepped toward her, still uncertain as to what he should say. The scolding he'd wanted to give her seemed inappropriate. Especially in light of his recent impulsive act.

"I'm a bit confused," he began. "The receptionist mentioned something about a quad bike."

It didn't make sense. This was Pricilla they were talking about.

Her gaze dropped to the floor. "If you want to know the truth, I borrowed. . .stole. . .an ATV from the shop down the road in order to follow my suspect."

Max shook his head. Surely he'd heard her wrong. "You did what?"

"It all made perfect sense at the time. The man was getting away and I was afraid I'd lose him."

"On an ATV?" She started toward the door and he hurried to catch up. Suddenly his escapade outside the bakery seemed tame. "You're sixty-five years old, Pricilla—"

"A fact that I don't need to be reminded of." She reached up and rubbed her shoulder with one hand. "I'm going to be sore for the next month."

"But on an ATV?" He still didn't believe her.

She stopped in front of the door and caught his gaze. "The man happened to be Kent Walters. Ezri's husband."

"Wait a minute? Ezri's husband?"

She held up the keys to her car and dangled them in front of his face. "Would you mind driving home? I'll tell you all about it on the way."

"Of course not." He closed his mouth. While she

might not have been entirely scrupulous in her behavior, from the looks of things, Pricilla had just discovered another twist in the case. Unlike himself, who'd dug up nothing more than a pile of unwanted junk mail.

She managed a half smile. "Thanks."

He held the door open for her then followed her out into the sunshine as she continued to ramble. She always rambled when she was nervous. Deciding not to try to get a word in, he simply listened as they walked the two blocks to where the car was parked.

Once he'd started the motor and pulled away, Pricilla's recap of what had happened only managed to raise his blood pressure a notch and solidify the thought that this time Pricilla had allowed her curiosity to get the best of her. And she seemed to have forgotten as well that, while her cat Penelope might have the fabled nine lives, as a woman of sixty-five she did not.

"I'm sorry about this whole mess." She let out a heavy sigh. "You were right. You're always right."

Perhaps she'd learned something from this experience after all.

"Right about what?" he prodded.

"You warned me that getting involved in this case would only get me into trouble."

"Pricilla—"

"But stealing a quad bike to chase down a suspect..." She shook her head. "This time I obviously went way too far."

He didn't say anything, still unsure as to how he should respond.

"So. . ." Pricilla blew out a sharp breath and kept

her gaze straight ahead.

"So what?"

She clasped her hands in her lap. "I thought you might have something scathing to say to reprimand me."

Following the curve of the road bordered by a row of pine trees, Max glanced at her out of the corner of his eye. He'd felt a bit guilty over ratting on Naldo for digging through the trash, though he had no plans at the moment of telling Pricilla what he'd been doing for the past hour. While he didn't believe the man's explanation, he was also pretty certain the incident didn't have anything to do with Reggie's murder. Pricilla, on the other hand, had been stalking suspects, stealing property, and interrogating innocent people—assuming Kent was innocent. The crazy thing about all of this was he knew that Pricilla would never hurt anyone intentionally. Not that motive always justified the actions, but in her case it couldn't help but push the scales slightly in her favor. He had to give her credit for that.

"Max?"

He needed to say something, but he still wasn't sure if he should laugh out loud or give her a good old-fashioned spanking. "I don't want you to think that just because I decided to take the next step and see where our relationship might be heading that I have some sort of control over you, but that doesn't change the fact that you've let your obsession with the case send you spiraling in the wrong direction."

"And. . ."

"And I'm worried that next time the outcome won't be in your favor."

Pricilla's fingernails gnawed on the door handle. "Don't get me wrong. I take full responsibility for my own actions, but that doesn't change the reality that something's not right with the case. Detective Carter is planning on arresting Annabelle."

While he couldn't ignore the fervor in her voice, that didn't justify the fact that if she didn't stay out of the detective's way, at some point she was going to find herself in serious trouble. And it scared him. "What if it's her son or Ezri who killed Reggie? Then what?"

Pricilla pursed her lips. "I'll accept the truth when it's finally revealed, but the man's got an agenda."

"Who?"

"The detective."

"And why do you think he has an agenda?"

"He wants to join the FBI."

Max frowned. "And that gives him an agenda?"

"Yes. . .no. . .I don't know, Max."

He pulled the car into the driveway of the lodge and parked beside a beat-up, two-door vehicle. "Promise me, agenda or not, that you'll stay out of this. Please."

Her lips smacked together. "I almost forgot."

"Forgot what?"

"That car must belong to Darren Robinson. I'd completely forgotten he promised me computer lessons today."

Max groaned inwardly. Here they went again. He knew that despite what had happened earlier today, Pricilla's agenda for computer lessons had little to do with learning to surf the Internet, and everything to do with assessing one of her suspects. And it was hardly a surprise that the appointment had slipped her mind between her unethical pursuit of Kent up the mountain and her subsequent visit to the detective's office.

"You promised to stay out of trouble, Pricilla," he warned.

She opened her door and scooted toward the edge. "Which is something I have every intention of doing. I'm only going to keep my eyes and ears open in case I stumble across any information relevant to the case. And even you have to admit that Darren Robinson is certainly relevant to the case."

Pricilla scooted her chair a couple of inches closer to the laptop so she could read the fuzzy screen that had just popped up. Darren might be charming and intelligent, but she wasn't going to let herself forget that he was a suspect in Reggie Pierce's murder.

She glanced at the young man sitting beside her at the kitchen table. His pressed khaki pants and button-down shirt looked sharp, and his manners were just as meticulous. Opportunity was the only thing she had on the young man, though. Reggie had given him a decent job, and he'd proved his worth in the business. Killing Reggie didn't make sense. But even if she didn't find any information to pass on to the detective regarding the case, she could always learn a thing or two about computers in the process.

"Mrs. Crumb?" The young man pushed his thick glasses up the bridge of his nose.

Whacking her leg on the edge of the table, Pricilla winced then forced herself away from her contemplations on the case and reminded herself why she was here.

"I'm sorry, Darren." She scrambled for a proper response. All she needed was for the young man to guess her real interest behind her request for a computer lesson. "Like I told you, the World Wide Web, and all aspects of computers for that matter, might as well be a language from an entirely different planet. My mind tends to. . .wander a tad."

"You're making it too complicated." His encouraging smile reached the corners of his hazel eyes, and she relaxed a bit. "A few simple guidelines and you can find out anything you want."

Pricilla determined to focus on the matter at hand, because there were a number of things she wanted to research once she learned to navigate the inner workings of modern technology. The detective's comment on Stewart dropping out of school for one, and Reggie's business background for another.

She drew in a deep breath. "How about showing me how to get to the bakery's Web site for starters?"

With a few clicks from Darren, a picture of the Baker's Dozen filled the screen. Pricilla studied the familiar storefront with its view of the Rocky Mountains in the background. The company logo crossed the top and a row of photos of bakery products edged the left side of the screen.

Darren leaned back. "You try it yourself now."

With Darren's encouragement and occasional instructions, Pricilla maneuvered through Italian pastries, specialty cakes, and mouthwatering chocolates, gaining confidence with every screen she opened. Maybe there was something to this computer craze after all. Shopping from the comfort of her own home would have its benefits, though perhaps not for her waistline or her pocketbook.

But she was interested in more than cream puffs and puff pastry. The more she knew about Reggie and his employees, the closer she would be to the answer behind the baker's fatal encounter.

An hour later Pricilla was still convinced Darren made it look far easier than it really was, but at least she could accomplish some of the basics. Being left alone to maneuver her way through the information would be a test she hoped she could pass, but either way, she was impressed with what she'd managed to learn.

She folded her hands in her lap, certain her brain would shut down if she had to think anymore today. "You're quite a wiz at this computer stuff."

"I spend more time in front of a screen than around people."

Pricilla decided to take the opening to find out more about the young man. "What about your family?"

"I don't see them much between school and work."

He pressed his hands against the table and sat up straight. His ease in communicating seemed to diminish as they switched to a personal subject. But Pricilla wanted to know more.

"Are you close to them?"

Darren scooted his chair back. "I'm an only child and my parents. . .well, let's just say they were never around much. Especially my father. Besides, I spent most of my life off at boarding school."

Darren's friendly smile melted into a deep frown that consumed his face and left a shadow across his eyes. She'd obviously hit upon a subject that he'd prefer to avoid.

Pricilla bit her lip and wondered how she always managed to hit a raw nerve. "I'm sorry. I didn't mean to bring up an unpleasant subject."

"No, it's fine. My father died a few years ago, then my mom remarried and now lives in Alaska. I'm pretty much on my own now." Darren's shrug was unconvincing. "None of us were ever particularly close. Like I said, my father was busy with work, and my mom. . ."

Darren clamped his mouth shut as if he'd said too much.

Pricilla decided she'd pressed the subject enough for now. "I'm sorry I brought up the subject, but I do appreciate all your help today."

She slid her chair back and stood to stretch her tight muscles while Darren gathered his cell phone and keys off the table without another word. She wasn't sure if she'd stumbled on something significant or simply a young man's loneliness.

She didn't want to read things into what he'd said, but his reaction did show that everyone has a secret, or at the least things they don't want to talk about. Darren Robinson might not be on the top of her suspect list, but until the killer confessed, she refused to eliminate any of them.

Max set his crossword puzzle on the arm of the porch chair and ran his fingers across the back of Penelope, Pricilla's Persian cat, who lay curled up contentedly in his lap. He had to chuckle to himself. The more he thought about it, the more he found humor in the entire four-wheeler escapade.

He squinted through the bright afternoon sunlight at the stunning backdrop of aspen and pine trees that surrounded the lodge. Truth be told, he'd have loved to see her scooting up the mountain behind the wheel of the ATV. Pricilla in a helmet with the wind blowing against the folds of her skirt as she sped across the rough terrain was a picture even he was finding hard to imagine. He couldn't help but chuckle out loud, but humorous antics aside, part of him wondered if she'd ever stop playing the role of detective and decide to settle down with him.

Not that he had ever expected her to get involved in yet another murder. And surely the odds of it ever happening again were slim to none. It wasn't as if she were Jessica Fletcher, whose scriptwriters ensured she encountered at least one dead body every episode. No, Pricilla was more like a twist on Hyacinth Bucket, PBS's unconventional busybody who'd somehow managed to trade in her guest list for a list of suspects.

Max scratched Penelope behind the ears and listened to the cat purr. If he was honest with himself, his plans to move to Colorado had been a spur-of-the-moment decision. No different, really, than Pricilla's impulsive act to chase after a murder victim in an off-road vehicle. Love, mystery, and old age all seemed to be factors in both of their madcap decisions.

He glanced up as Pricilla strolled across the porch with a plate of brownies in one hand and a tall glass of milk in the other. The brownies were no doubt a peace offering, and one he would accept with no qualms. No matter what she did, he couldn't deny the fact that he loved Pricilla and couldn't stay annoyed at her for too long. Pricilla was. . .well. . .Pricilla, and the enthusiastic way she faced life was part of what he loved about her. It just happened to be the part that most often got her in trouble.

She set the dessert and glass of milk on a small side table beside his padded chair and shot him a smile. "Are you still mad at me?"

He took the largest brownie off the plate and cocked his head. "For some strange reason, you're hard to stay mad at."

She slid into the chair beside him and reached out to squeeze his free hand. "I know I've been a bit obsessed with the case and trying to prove that Annabelle is innocent, but I never should have let things get out of hand like they did today."

"You're a good friend, Pricilla." He laced her fingers between his as he took a nibble of the rich chocolate. "No one could ever deny that fact."

She didn't look convinced. "Being a good friend doesn't excuse the fact that I foolishly embarked on a reckless escapade that could have had serious consequences. Both physical and legal."

"That's true, but no one will ever doubt that your motives are pure."

"Pure motives don't justify illegal actions." Pricilla grabbed one of the brownies and took a big bite.

Max stifled a laugh at the intensity in her voice, knowing that no matter what he said, it was going to take more than his encouragement and a chocolate brownie to ease Pricilla's guilt in this situation. "That might be true, but even a court of law takes into consideration the reasoning behind an act when pronouncing judgment."

"So you're trying to tell me that the motives behind my actions excuse or even justify what I did?"

"I'm trying to tell you to stop being so hard on yourself. We all make mistakes."

"I agree with that." She wiped a crumb off the front of her dress. "It's interesting. At Reggie's funeral I remember talking to Annabelle about how we are all weak vessels. Paul describes us as jars of clay. My point was that although we can be crushed from life's circumstances, we are not destroyed. At that point, though, I was thinking about how Annabelle's entire life had changed in one moment, but it applies to all of us."

"And makes you realize not only how worthless man really is, but how Christ changed all of that through His death on the cross." He reached for his milk and took a sip. "It always amazes me that it's through the trials and tribulations we face that God's glory is the most apparent."

"How do I make Annabelle understand that?"

"By believing it first yourself."

"Ouch." She winced at his answer. "Touché."

"I'm sorry—"

"No, you're right. It's a lesson I have to take to heart before I can ever make someone else understand."

Somehow, he had no doubts that she would take it to heart. "By the way, how did the computer lesson go? I've been wondering where you were. Darren left close to an hour ago."

"I decided to put what I learned into practice and 'surf the Web,' as they say, for a while."

He glanced at her out of the corner of his eye as he took a bite of his brownie and frowned. She'd forced too much enthusiasm into that last sentence. Something was afoot.

"Pricilla?"

"Yes?"

Her response came far too quickly. The brownies were more than a peace offering. They were smoothing out the edges for what was to come.

He set his glass down and caught her gaze. "You found out something, didn't you?"

"I know I promised to stay out of the investigation, but even the detective said if I happened to hear something or—"

"Purposefully stumble across something on the Web?" Had she learned nothing from her recent madcap adventure?

"All I wanted to do was try out some of the things Darren taught me. I thought I would Google a few names—"

"Google a few names?"

"You might not find all of this quite so humorous when you find out what I discovered."

Max drew in a deep breath. "Humorous" wasn't at all what he would call the situation. "I'm listening."

"Reggie Pierce used to own an upscale restaurant in New York." Pricilla leaned forward and looked at him intently. "Annabelle mentioned it a few times, but from what I read, even her descriptions didn't do it justice. I'd always assumed that the pressure of running such an upscale venture became too much, and Reggie wanted a slower pace. Now I'm not so sure."

He had to admit his own growing sense of curiosity, though he'd never admit it to Pricilla. "Why's that?"

Her eyes widened. "Seven years ago Reggie's business partner died under mysterious circumstances. And the overall consensus is that he was murdered."

Pricilla stepped out of the warm sunshine and into the air-conditioned climate of the bakery. Breathing deeply, she let the savory scents of yeast bread and sweet chocolate fill her lungs. Ezri stood behind the counter, filling an order for a mother with two small children in tow. While Ezri's taste in clothes ran along the lines of eccentric with her vintage fringe vest and embroidered black jeans, today there was something different about her. Her smile was broader, and there was a lilt to her voice.

"Mrs. Crumb. It's so good to see you." Ezri waved a pair of metal tongs in Pricilla's direction. "I'll be with you in just a moment."

"No hurry." Pricilla crossed the checkered tiled floor, stopping in front of the glass-covered pastries. "It will give me time to decide what I need this morning."

Breakfast had been hours ago. A blueberry muffin would hold her over until lunchtime and certainly wouldn't do too much damage to her waistline. On the other hand, the éclairs looked extra good today.

Two minutes later the bell at the front door jingled as the mother bustled her children outside, their angelic faces covered with chocolate from their pastries.

Pricilla eyed the fresh loaves of bread that would go perfectly with tonight's dinner of beef medallions and roasted vegetables and made her decision. She tapped on the glass. "I'll take five loaves of the sourdough and one of your strawberry cheesecakes. I thought an extra dessert during coffee would be nice for the guests."

"A perfect choice, Mrs. Crumb." Ezri grabbed a sack from the counter that had the Baker's Dozen's logo printed across the top.

Pricilla studied the row of pastries for a second time and couldn't resist. Blueberry muffins were good, but the éclairs looked irresistible. It was too bad Annabelle owned a bakery and not a health food store. "And you can throw in two of your cream-filled éclairs for me as well."

Pricilla didn't miss the sparkle in Ezri's eyes as she slid the first mouthwatering éclair into a small white box, but she was quite certain that the young woman's beaming smile had nothing to do with éclairs.

Still, before she went any further with her questions, she had a confession to make. "I never was able to apologize to you for what happened yesterday—"

"Trust me, Mrs. Crumb. You don't owe me an apology." Ezri set the box down and leaned against the display counter. The grin never left her face as she held out her hand, showing off the diamond wedding ring that encircled her finger.

"Why, Ezri, it's stunning." Pricilla studied the young woman's pear-shaped diamond and felt a wave of relief flood through her. Maybe something good had come out of yesterday's fiasco. "So you told your mother?"

Ezri pressed her hand against her heart. "I've never been so relieved about anything in my entire life. There are no secrets about Kent and our marriage anymore. And it's all due to you."

"I don't know that I deserve any of the credit." Pricilla ran her fingers across the empty space on her own left hand. For months after Marty's death she'd continued to wear the ring he'd given her decades before. The day she finally laid it to rest in the back of her jewelry box had brought with it a flurry of emotions, and while she still missed the ring on her finger, now she could only think of Max and wonder if she was ready to accept such a commitment from him.

Ezri rested her hands against the counter. "Trust me, Mrs. Crumb. If it wasn't for your showing up yesterday and knocking some sense into me, I'd still be trying to live a double life."

Shoving aside her own relationship questions, Pricilla tried to focus on the matter at hand. "What does your mother think about Kent?"

Ezri slid a loaf of bread into a sack. "Besides the adjustment to knowing that her little girl is married, I think she's happy. She seems to like Kent and knows that he makes me happy. I never should have kept it a secret, but at least things seem to have worked out finally."

"I'm really happy for you, Ezri. You've been through a lot lately and the last thing you need is the stress of keeping more secrets."

Ezri nodded toward the back of the bakery. "My mother's upstairs, and I know she'd love to see you. I can finish getting your order boxed up and have it waiting for you."

Pricilla nodded, but her stomach recoiled at the reason she needed to see Annabelle. Things had worked out for Ezri and Kent, but what was going to happen if the detective dragged Annabelle off to jail and managed to slap her with a murder conviction? Ezri might have Kent to give her a sense of stability, but the two of them should be enjoying life as newlyweds, not having to deal with the reality of Annabelle's possible prison sentence.

And what about Stewart? At twenty years old, he still had a lot of growing up to do. With the little she knew about the young man, it seemed obvious that losing a second parent could be permanently detrimental.

Pricilla trembled at the thought. She had to find out the truth. "I had planned to go see your mother, but I wondered if I could ask you something first."

"Of course."

Pricilla paused for a moment as Detective Carter's harsh words of warning repeated themselves in her mind. No. All she was doing was taking advantage of the opportunity, something he had grudgingly given her permission to do. Certainly there was nothing wrong with that.

Pricilla cleared her throat. "I know this is none of my business, but I can't help but be worried about your brother. I understand he dropped out of school?"

Ezri's smile vanished. "He didn't kill our father—"

"I know." Pricilla held up her hand. "I'd never accuse him of murder, Ezri. That wasn't my intention. But I am concerned."

Ezri slipped another loaf of bread into the sack. "I have to admit I'm worried, too. I'm not positive, but I'm pretty sure he's run up a lot of debt. Please don't tell my mother. If anyone should be cured of keeping secrets, it's me, but I don't know what to do, and until I have proof. . ."

Pricilla shook her head. "Your mother needs to know, Ezri. The detective is aware that your brother dropped out of school, and if there's debt involved, he probably already knows. It's always better to simply come clean."

Ezri stared at the rows of baked goods in front of her, her face now void of the joy it had held only moments before. "I heard them fighting a few weeks back because dad wouldn't give him any extra money. Stewart liked to live well, but frankly, he's lazy."

"Laziness isn't a motive for murder, but I am concerned how the detective will look at things. He's determined to wrap up this case, and the last thing I want is your mother or your brother—"

"We both know my mother didn't have anything to do with my father's death." Ezri's voice rose a notch. "And neither did my brother, Mrs. Crumb. I'm certain of it. Stewart might be lazy and even a bit irresponsible, but he's not a murderer."

Pricilla covered the young woman's hand with her own and squeezed gently, wishing she could give her more assurances. "I'm going to do everything I can to help, Ezri. I promise."

A moment later Pricilla took the narrow flight of steps to the upstairs apartment. There was no getting around the facts. If Stewart had known that his father had been in the process of cutting him out of his will, then he had the perfect motivation for murder.

Pricilla found Annabelle sitting at an antique desk with a pen in her hand, staring at a blank card. The grieving woman didn't even move as one of the wooden floor boards in the living room creaked beneath Pricilla's weight.

Pricilla paused at the edge of the oriental rug. There had been no attempts made to tidy the normally organized room. Papers were scattered across the floor. Three empty pizza boxes lay discarded on the dining room table. Even the sink was full of dirty dishes.

"Annabelle?"

Annabelle continued staring at the card. "I need to send thank-you notes to people. Reggie didn't have a lot of friends, but there were flowers and cards. His aunt who's almost ninety even sent five hundred dollars for the kids' education."

Pricilla raised her eyebrows. "That was generous."

"It was very nice of her, wasn't it? Except five hundred dollars won't even pay for one class." She shook her head and looked up for the first time. "I'm sorry—"

Pricilla bridged the gap between them and rested her hand on Annabelle's shoulder. Her friend's normal stylish attire had been discarded for old jeans and a T-shirt, matching the disheveled room. "You don't ever have to be sorry for grieving. It's a natural part of the process."

"I know, but I had been feeling better. I've been thinking about what we talked about. How I need to

let God forgive me and allow Him to give me strength."
She pointed to a Bible that lay open to the book of
Philippians. "I read this morning how Paul says that
Christ will take our weak mortal bodies and change
them into glorious bodies like His own."

"It's a beautiful passage, isn't it?"

"Yes, but then it keeps hitting me again. Reggie's
dead, and all the detective's evidence is pointing at me,
which means I'll probably end up being arrested." She
caught Pricilla's gaze. "You believe that I'm innocent,
don't you, Pricilla?"

"That's why I'm here."

Annabelle reached out to squeeze Pricilla's hand
and let a smile cross her lips for the first time. "I don't
know what I'd do without you."

"What I want you to do right now is go sit on the
couch, and I'll make you some tea."

"I'd like that." Annabelle dropped the pen, which
slid off the desk and onto the floor, but she didn't
bother to pick it up. "I need to tell you something first,
though. It's about Ezri."

"She showed me her ring." Pricilla bustled into the
kitchen that opened into the living room, and filled
the teapot with water from the tap. "Are you doing
okay after finding out about her marriage?"

Annabelle labored across the room before stopping
to lean against the back of the couch. "In not knowing
what's going to happen to me, I'm relieved she has someone who will take care of her."

"We're going to find out the truth, Annabelle."

Annabelle sighed audibly. "Sometimes I'm not

sure that discovering the truth is the best thing."

Pricilla looked up from the granite counter where she was assembling the milk and sugar and paused to look at her friend. Women in the church had organized a few meals after the funeral, but Annabelle was too high-strung this morning and probably hadn't eaten anything decent for days despite the offered help. "Can I make you some toast or an omelet?"

Annabelle shook her head. "Tea is fine, thank you."

Pricilla pulled out a pair of mugs from the cupboard and decided she wouldn't leave until the dishes were done and she'd helped to catch up on some of the housekeeping. "What did you want to talk to me about?"

Annabelle pressed her hands against her heart. "It seems that the detective is digging into everything I've ever said or done until he finds that final piece of evidence that will put me away for life."

"He is persistent, but in all honesty, I think he only wants to find the truth." Pricilla located the box of tea bags, surprised she'd just defended the detective. Perhaps seeing the photo of his wife and daughter had added a bit of humanity to the balding lawman.

Annabelle shoved back a strand of her bleached hair that was beginning to show streaks of gray.

"You need to relax, Annabelle."

"I know, but I have to show you something." She pulled something out of the back of the desk drawer then perched on the edge of the bar stool facing the kitchen.

She slapped a photo on the bar and pushed it toward

Pricilla. "This is Riley Folk. Ezri's biological father."

Pricilla dropped the saucer she was holding against the counter. She moved to catch it, but instead the small plate cracked in two against the hard surface. "I'm sorry."

"Forget about it."

Pricilla held up the broken pieces. "I just. . .I had no idea you were married before—"

"I wasn't. I learned the hard way that secrets cause nothing but trouble in the end. Reggie found out the day before he died."

"I. . .I don't know what to say."

Pricilla turned away to dump the broken pieces of the saucer into the trash can. Max had tried to tell her that everyone has secrets, but she'd refused to believe that Annabelle had any secrets—or at least any secrets worth murdering for. But hidden beneath the polished exterior of their marriage had been at least one skeleton

Annabelle fingered the photo. "I've always been ashamed of what happened. Reggie never knew until he found this picture."

Pricilla studied the picture of the man. "Who was Riley?"

"No one, really." Annabelle shrugged. "A man who happened to fill my loneliness while Reggie worked late hours. I finally broke it off, but when Ezri was born there was no doubt in my mind who the father was. Blond hair, blue eyes. . .Reggie never suspected a thing."

The teakettle whistled, and Pricilla was thankful for the distraction. She knew Annabelle had regrets in her past, but she'd never expected something like this. She was always amazed at people who balked at the morality of the Bible without considering the heaviness of sin's consequences—like the ones Annabelle had been living with and would continue to live with for the rest of her life.

Pushing all doubts of Annabelle's innocence aside, Pricilla poured the hot water into the tea cups and slid one across the bar to Annabelle. "I have to say, I'm not sure I understand why you wanted to tell me. Does this have something to do with Reggie's death?"

Annabelle grasped her cup with two hands. "I don't know if it has anything to do with it or not, but something else is bothering me. You know how Reggie was impulsive about keeping everything in perfect order. He even kept his sock drawer color-coordinated." She waved her arm toward the messy living area. "As you can see, his tidiness never completely rubbed off on me, but I always tried to keep things clean. Anyway, lately he started blaming me for various things that were out of place. I'd noticed it too, but it wasn't me. Every once in a while I'd find things moved around the house. Little things that I never would have noticed except for Reggie's idiosyncrasies to have everything in its exact spot. It was how he found the photo, trying to figure out what else was out of place."

Pricilla worked to fit the pieces together, but inevitably something was missing. "I'm not sure how all of this fits together, but since we're talking about secrets, I do have a question for you."

Annabelle took a sip of her tea. "Ask me anything. I'm tired of secrets and am determined not to keep any more."

Pricilla decided to be completely forthright. "All right then. I'm curious about Reggie's previous business partner, William Roberts. I'm only bringing up the subject because anything I can find out about, the detective is sure to find out about as well, if he hasn't already."

"I'm not sure that there's a whole lot to tell. Reggie and William owned a successful restaurant in New York. Reggie's plan was always to make it big, then eventually retire to the mountains in Colorado and start a bakery, which is exactly what he ended up doing. The restaurant did very well until William's death. Reggie was good at investing in a number of diverse markets with his profits. Stocks, bonds, art, even jewelry. He was ruthless in business and always did whatever it took to get ahead."

"How did William die? The article I read wasn't conclusive."

Annabelle shrugged. "That's because we never really knew what happened. The police finally decided that his death was a suicide, but I'm not sure. He didn't seem like the kind of man who would kill himself. It was a strange time. The restaurant began to suffer with the bad publicity, so Reggie decided to pull out while things were still ahead and moved us all here."

"Sounds like that might have been the best thing, considering the circumstances."

"I've always felt a bit guilty, though." Annabelle rested her tea on the counter. "We didn't even attend William's funeral. Our entire family came down with a case of the flu. It was horrible. William's wife and her son left immediately after the funeral and headed for her parents' home on Nantucket Island. Not that the two of us were close, but I never saw her again."

"I think we've talked enough about the past for today." Pricilla noted the dark circles under Annabelle's eyes, even more noticeable against her pallid skin color. "There is only one thing you can do right now, Annabelle."

"What is that?"

"You need to continue searching to rediscover God's love. He's the only one who will never let you down. And the one place where you will be able to find the strength to make it through this difficult time."

An hour later, with the kitchen cleaned and the living room tidied, Pricilla made her way back down the staircase from Annabelle's apartment toward her car, still trying to ignore nigglings of doubt in the back of her mind. The last thing she wanted to believe was that Annabelle could have been involved in something as horrid as murder. But she also knew that life with Reggie could be unbearable. There was one looming reality she couldn't shake. He'd discovered a shocking secret and had threatened to leave her out of his will.

And now Annabelle was free.

14

Pricilla hammered the blade of the knife into the carrot like a machete flying through the overgrowth of a dense jungle. She needed to have dinner ready for the lodge's guests in thirty minutes, but all she could think about was Annabelle and her confession.

Max stood beside her at the counter, roped into chopping tomatoes and yellow peppers for the salad because Misty had needed to take her youngest daughter to the doctor. Thankfully, everything else for the three-course meal was ready.

Pricilla picked up another carrot and started chopping again despite twinges of arthritis that told her to slow down and continue at a reasonable pace.

Max reached out and covered Pricilla's hand before sliding the butcher knife away from her. "You're hacking at these carrots like they're a troop of enemy soldiers coming at you. You're going to cut one of your fingers off."

Pricilla held up her hands in defeat. "I'm sorry. My mind is a million miles away right now."

"Or more precisely in the town of Rendezvous at a quaint little bakery?"

Pricilla frowned. "I wish I could tell you everything Annabelle shared with me—"

"What you and Annabelle discussed needs to stay between you and Annabelle, but that doesn't change the fact that I am concerned. You're too caught up in this case for your own good."

"I'm fine, Max. Really. Right now all we need to be worried about is Annabelle." Pricilla dumped the carrots into the salad bowl then rested her hands against the counter. "She's the one facing time in prison if new evidence doesn't show up."

Max added the tomatoes he'd chopped to the bowl. "I know Annabelle is a good friend of yours, and that you're determined to find out the truth, but I think you need to prepare yourself for the reality that she might have been involved. She, above anyone else, seems to have the perfect motive."

Pricilla squeezed her eyes shut, hating the fact that Max was right. Already, she'd discovered enough secrets in that family to sink the *Titanic*, and if truth be told, any one of them could have been a part of it.

"'He reveals deep and hidden things; he knows what lies in darkness, and light dwells with him.'" She blew out a labored breath, mulling over the words from Daniel for the second time since her morning devotional. "Why does it seem that the older I get, the more questions I have for God? Not that I doubt His authority and sovereignty, but I do question man's consistent weakness."

Max went back to work on chopping a pepper. "It's a tough question that only God truly understands. He might have created man in His image, but He also gave us choices. That's what makes us human."

"Humans who, more often than not, seem to choose the wrong direction that in turn causes a domino effect of consequences." Pricilla picked up her notebook from the counter and flipped it open. "Speaking of consequences, I've added at least one new motive. Stewart dropped out of school and his father refused to give him the money he wanted. Add to that, Ezri is pretty certain he's run up debt that he can't pay off."

Pricilla didn't feel comfortable mentioning Annabelle's indiscretions at this point, though she knew that if the facts continued to implicate her friend, the detective would need to know the truth. For now, though, she'd continue praying that her instincts were right, and that Annabelle's moments of carelessness years earlier hadn't led her to make an even bigger mistake with Reggie.

Max snatched the notebook out of her hands. "I thought the incident with that ATV had cured you of your involvement, Pricilla."

"It cured me of doing something foolish without thinking through the consequences. Even the detective is open to my input as long as I pass any information on to him."

"Input that you might happen to stumble across, not information you seek out."

Pricilla ignored the warning. "I need to talk to Stewart."

"And you really believe that Detective Carter won't put you behind bars for meddling in his case?"

"Don't be ridiculous. Nothing like that will happen again." She held up her hand. "No more four-wheelers. Scout's honor."

Max's laugh surprised her. He grabbed her hands before pulling them against his chest. "How can it be that the very thing I love the most about you, your care and compassion for others, happens to also be the one thing that gets you into the most trouble?"

"At least you're able to see the good side of my somewhat suspect character traits." Looking into his blue eyes, all the doubts she'd harbored regarding their relationship began to slip. Max was the one person who continued to believe in her no matter what.

"And where do you think we might find Stewart?" she asked him.

"Ezri said he spends most of his time hanging out at the pool hall."

"You'll come with me?"

Max shot her a grin. "Someone needs to keep you out of trouble. And besides that, the sooner this case is solved, the sooner we can start making progress on our relationship."

Max stepped into the darkened pool hall behind Pricilla and wondered if he'd been too quick to offer her help on her mission to question Stewart. Not that the atmosphere was as bad as he'd imagined. The setting seemed to be more of a hangout for young people than a smoky bar for brawling hoodlums, but he still felt out of his element. Loud music played in the background. Some boys' band with repetitive lyrics he couldn't understand. Even the pungent smells from the kitchen were geared toward the younger crowed with its heart-attack-inducing greasy choices, which he avoided—like French fries and fried burgers.

He hated feeling his age.

"There he is."

Max glanced in the direction Pricilla pointed. Stewart leaned against the wall with a pool cue in one hand and a bottle of water in the other. At least the young man didn't appear to be drinking alcohol.

Max squinted across the room at Stewart. After their last interview with him, Max wasn't sure he wanted to go another round. He turned back to Pricilla. "What are you going to do? Offer to play a round of pool with him?"

"Of course not." Pricilla flashed him an annoyed look. "That would be ridiculous. And besides, do you actually think he would agree to play with me? I've never touched one of these poles in my life."

"It's a pool cue."

"Whatever." The look of determination in Pricilla's eyes had yet to waver. "That's why you're going to offer."

"I'm going to what?" Max choked on the words.

"It's a perfect plan. We need a way to get him to relax and trust us."

"I haven't played pool for years—"

Pricilla frowned and rested her hands on her hips. "I've seen that trophy you won."

"From 1967!"

"You'll do fine."

Pricilla was already halfway across the tiled floor by the time Max recovered his bearings. A little friendly competition during his early military days couldn't begin to have any impact on what might happen today if he attempted to play a game of pool. Besides, with Pricilla instigating one question after another to the poor chap, it hardly seemed like a way to get the young man to relax and open up.

"Max." Pricilla waved at him from the other side of the room.

Max made his way past cracked vinyl chairs and small, round tables and wondered if he would set off an alarm escaping through the emergency exit to his left. Why did his intentions to be the gallant hero in helping Pricilla with her oddball quests always seem to land him in a boiling pot of trouble? He had no doubt that that was exactly where this innocent escapade was headed.

As promised, Pricilla greeted the young man then suggested a friendly game of pool between the two men.

Stewart slouched against the wall. "I was waiting for friends, but they're late."

Max seized his one way out. "We don't have to play—"

"Max." Pricilla's gaze bore through him, more pointed than the end of a pool cue.

Max rephrased his sentence. "You don't mind?"

Stewart tossed the empty plastic water bottle into the trash and shrugged. "Beats doing nothing."

The young man positioned the balls on the table and racked them up. Max grabbed a pool cue and chalked the end, wondering if he could come up with a last minute reprieve. A quick glance at Pricilla reminded him of her determination. Her mind was made up, and leaving now would only result in having to defend himself later. Something he'd prefer not to do.

With her notebook peeking out from her jacket pocket, all she needed was Columbo's trench coat and she'd fit the part of detective to a T. And like Columbo, she didn't seem to have any intention of waiting to toss out the first question. "Your mother told me that you were studying forensic science. Is that right? It sounds like such a fascinating subject to me."

Stewart shrugged as he lined up his pool cue for the opening shot. "Some of the classes have been interesting. Beats working in a bakery all summer long."

"What classes will you be taking next semester?"

Stewart's staid expression never changed. "Not sure if I'm going back."

Max took his turn at the table and somehow managed to drop a solid ball into a corner pocket.

Stewart stood up straight for the first time and nodded his head. "Not bad for an old man."

Max lined up for another shot and decided to take the young man's words as a compliment. "Thanks."

He frowned as another ball hit the side of the table and bounced away from the pocket he'd been aiming at. Pricilla wasn't going to hear the end of this. He was sacrificing his pride for the sake of her investigation. She'd better come up with some answers. Fast.

In the meantime, though, it might not hurt to do some of the talking himself. It was going to take more than chitchat to break the ice between them. "It took me awhile to find out what I wanted to do with my life. After two semesters of classes at a community college down in New Mexico, I dropped out of school against my father's wishes."

He avoided Pricilla's gaze. Perhaps his line of questioning wasn't going in the direction she'd planned, but if she intended to drop any bombshell questions regarding Reggie's death, she was going to need all the warming up possible.

Stewart grabbed some chalk from a ledge along the wall. "What did you end up doing?"

"I joined the military."

"Whoa. That would be way too much discipline for me."

Max studied his next shot, wishing he'd done better in geometry. Mathematics and angles had never been his forte. "I'm certainly not saying that the military is for everyone, but I do believe that it's perfectly normal to take time to discover what you want to do for the rest of your life. For me, though, the military became exactly that. I eventually learned to negotiate, plan strategic campaigns for the military attacks, and even interrogate prisoners."

"Really?" Admiration dawned in the young man's eyes. Maybe they were making progress after all.

Max pulled back his pool cue and clipped his intended ball too far to the right. "It might not have taught me all the skills I need for a game of pool. . ."

Stewart laughed as he approached the table for his turn.

". . .but it did teach me discipline along with essential life skills that I would have been able to use whether I'd served only one term or made serving my country a lifetime career."

Max winked at Pricilla, whose smile of thanks sent a shiver of emotions running through him. Perched atop the vinyl bar stool, she looked prettier than any of the twenty-something girls who sat laughing too loudly at one of the back tables. Pricilla's silver hair lay in perfect curls against the nape of her neck, and her face, with just a hint of makeup, still looked fresh. The years might have added a few wrinkles, but they had brought with them an extra dose of grace and charm, and he still found her beautiful.

Maybe being over the hill wasn't so bad after all.

Stewart paused at the corner of the table. "I've always wanted to run my own business."

"You're in the perfect position then." Pricilla's voice competed against the background music. "The Baker's Dozen has potential for growth, and you've got the opportunity to learn how it works from the ground up."

Stewart didn't look convinced. "Working the cash register and filling boxes with donuts isn't exactly running a business."

"My experience with negotiations and interrogations didn't happen overnight. It never does. I first had to survive boot camp then work my way up the ladder." Max sank a clean shot. "It's the same with anything. You've got to prove yourself and pay your dues. In the end, though, it's worth it."

"I suppose you've got a point."

"Have you ever thought about helping your mother run the bakery someday?" Pricilla's question was met with serious contemplation from Stewart.

"I don't want anything to do with the bakery."

"Why not?"

"Why should I? I've already told you how my father cared more about his work than he ever did about his family." Stewart's pool cue scraped against the green felt as he scratched the shot. "I don't owe him anything."

Pricilla slid off the stool and moved to stand beside the pool table. "Who do you think killed him?"

The bottom of Stewart's pool cue hit the ground. Pricilla had asked one question too many, taking her friendly chat to the despised level of an interrogation.

"That old detective sent you back to get more information out of me, didn't he?"

"Trust me, Stewart." Max tried not to laugh at the image. "Detective Carter would quit before he ever gave Pricilla a badge and sent her out on an investigation. Pricilla's concerned for your family. That's all."

Pricilla cleared her throat. "And considering how the last time we talked you practically confessed to murdering your father—"

"I didn't confess to anything."

"True, but you were the one willing to give us both a motive and an opportunity."

"If you're digging for evidence, I'll give you more." Stewart dropped a striped ball into a hole, then lined up for another shot. "Two months ago I dropped out of school. Never told my dad. I knew he'd cut me off entirely if he ever found out that I was spending his money without earning a single hour of college credit.

"That was the problem with him. As long as we did what he wanted, he never bothered us. He chose the classes on forensic science for me with some sort of unreasonable expectations that I'd become a doctor or a top FBI agent. He never asked me what I wanted to do with my life." The veins in Stewart's neck began to bulge as he sank another ball into a corner pocket. "And if he knew the truth. . ."

Pricilla took a step closer to the table. "What is the truth, Stewart?"

"The truth? Is that what you want to know? How about the fact that I've run up more debt than the bakery brings in in a year? I tried to tell him that I was in trouble the week before he died. But do you think he cared, or would even listen to me?"

"Your father loved you, Stewart."

"Really? Funny. I never saw it, yet still I thought maybe, just maybe, he'd treat me like his son one day. Not that I expected him to welcome me with open arms and a big party, but I thought he'd at least hear me out." Stewart grasped his pool cue with both hands and split it in two across his leg. "Right before he died, he threatened to cut me out of his will. Something he obviously would have followed through with if someone hadn't killed him."

"Stewart." Max took a step closer. "This isn't going to help."

The owner of the establishment stepped out from behind the counter. "Young man, I'd suggest you stop right now, or I'm going to call the sheriff."

Stewart threw a cue ball toward the owner, barely missing Pricilla in the process. Instead it shattered a glass case behind the counter. "You wanted more evidence, didn't you? What are you thinking right now? Reckless son murders his father in order to get his hands on his inheritance. It fits, doesn't it?"

"Stewart." Max grabbed the broken stick out of the young man's hand, then looked up as Detective Carter stepped into the room. With the broken cue stick in his hands and Pricilla's recent exploits, he was quite certain this wasn't going to look good to the detective.

"I can't believe this." The balding officer stomped across the floor. "I was walking by and happened to hear a bit of ruckus. I want all three of you to come with me down to the station. Now."

"But I—"

"Yes, you too, Mrs. Crumb. I would have thought that our talk yesterday would have made more of an impact on you. Stealing a four-wheeler and now a barroom brawl."

"Detective Carter." Pricilla's face had turned an ashen shade of gray. "I will not have my name marred with untrue facts."

Max grimaced at her attempts to clear her good name. So much for her promises that nothing like this would ever happen again. Innocent or not, Pricilla was being hauled down to the sheriff's office for disturbing the peace. And he was going with her.

15

Pricilla sat with her hands in her lap in Detective Carter's now familiar office. The two glass walls seemed to close in on her. The detective stood, leaning against his desk with an unmistakable scowl written across his face. Max sat hunched down in his chair beside her as if he wished he could disappear into the floor boards. That was something she'd like to do at the moment as well.

Carter pulled the small notebook and pen from his shirt pocket. "Before I go and talk to Stewart, I wanted to see the two of you alone."

"This is all an innocent misunderstanding, Detective. . ."

Pricilla paused, afraid that anything she said would only make things worse. She might not have participated in Stewart's bout of temper, but in reality she had instigated it with her pointed questions. The young man had been on the edge of exploding, and she'd managed to add fuel to the flame.

"It goes beyond an innocent misunderstanding, Mrs. Crumb, when we're looking at over three hundred dollars in damages. I want to know what happened." The detective folded his arms across his chest. "Surely you weren't back on the sleuthing trail, now, were you?"

Pricilla swallowed hard. "I was worried about Stewart. As a friend."

"Worried?" The detective didn't seem pleased with

her answer. "And why were you worried?"

Pricilla glanced at Max, who had yet to say a word. He avoided her gaze. "I suppose it will all come out in the end, so there's no use in keeping any secrets."

"No, there isn't." Detective Carter shoved his glasses up the bridge of his nose, then poised his pen to write. "Keeping secrets would mean that not only did you go beyond our agreement to cross-examine Stewart—"

"We weren't cross-examining Stewart—"

". . .it would also mean that you didn't pass along vital information to me regarding my ongoing investigation." He ignored her input and tapped on the notebook. "There's a name for that, you know. Withholding evidence."

"I get the point." Pricilla squirmed in her chair. "First of all, Stewart dropped out of school two months ago."

The detective didn't look impressed. "I am aware of that fact, Mrs. Crumb. I told you that the last time you were here."

"I know."

She fiddled with her purse strap, wishing there was a way out of spilling the information she had. Max had warned her that her probing would get her into trouble, and as always, he'd been right. Only now she'd dragged him into the situation as an accomplice.

She stared at the lined patterns on the tiled floor. "There is more."

"Good, because at the moment that's the only thing keeping you out of a jail cell."

"Detective Carter." Max spoke up for the first time,

exasperation filling his voice. "Both you and I know that you have nothing on either Pricilla or me that would merit holding us in a jail cell. I'd appreciate it if you'd avoid using theatrics in this interview."

"Fine." The detective shrugged. "Please continue, Mrs. Crumb. Out of respect for justice in this situation, since we've now had to rule out jail time."

While she might dislike the detective's methods, she couldn't help but smile at Max's attempt to save her honor. Carter's sullen expression emphasized the fact that he wasn't happy with either one of them at the moment, but perhaps all wasn't lost. And one thing was for certain. She was done probing for evidence in this case. No more Holmes and Watson. No more interviews, questions, or digging for the truth, since all she ever seemed to manage was soiling her own reputation.

"Mrs. Crumb."

"I'm sorry." She worked to focus on the issue at hand. "Apparently Stewart has been involved in some sort of gambling and has racked up quite a large debt."

"How much?"

"I don't know exactly, though I'd venture to guess that the figures are substantial. Five or six figures perhaps?"

The detective whistled under his breath. "That is substantial. What else?"

While Pricilla didn't like where the conversation was going, she knew she had no choice but to come clean on what she'd learned. "Stewart came to his father about a week before Reggie was killed and asked for money."

"Hmmm. . ." Carter rubbed his chin. "Now this

is getting interesting. You might have just won a free get-out-of-jail card."

Max cleared his throat.

"Sorry." The detective scribbled some more notes. "What else do you have?"

"Nothing really, except for the fact that Reggie and Stewart did have a big fight, and Stewart threatened to take him out of his will."

"That's certainly not nothing. We know that Reggie planned to follow through with cutting the entire family out of his will. That leaves us with a bottom line that Stewart now has motive and opportunity."

Pricilla felt her stomach lurch. "I never meant to imply that the boy killed his father—"

"You didn't have to. The evidence always speaks loud and clear on its own."

Pricilla felt forced to backpedal away from the hole she'd just dug for herself. And Stewart. "Certainly he has a temper and needs to grow up, but my gut tells me that he's innocent."

"Like Annabelle?"

"Yes, like Annabelle. . ."

Pricilla closed her mouth. Gut feelings weren't going to get her anywhere in this office. How could she explain, using evidence, that she believed something—or someone else—had to be involved? Even she couldn't come to that conclusion with the evidence she'd gathered. The truth was, she simply didn't want Annabelle to suffer any more than she already had. Stewart's conviction would hurt Annabelle more than if she herself was sent to prison. There was no way around the facts, though. Stewart had both motive and opportunity, whether she liked it or not.

Pricilla uncrossed her legs and slid forward in her chair, ready to leave. "Can we go now?"

"After my required lecture. You know I'm not happy with either of you." His thick glasses had slipped down the bridge of his nose, giving him the air of a disgruntled professor. He shoved them back into place with his forefinger.

She was getting tired of defending herself. "We had nothing to do with the broken pool cue or the broken glass—"

The detective held up his hand. "Nevertheless, I was forced to arrest you yesterday, and now you've been involved, innocent or not, with a brawl at the pool hall. Hardly behavior for one of the leading figures of our community."

Pricilla frowned, certain that the detective's comment was meant in jest.

But the detective didn't look amused. "I suppose a thank-you is in order, though. With the evidence I've already collected on Stewart, I now have enough to go to the DA."

"What about Annabelle?"

"Let's just say that I'm not completely eliminating any family members at this point." The detective shoved his notebook and pen back into his front pocket. "And Mrs. Crumb?"

"Yes?"

"In the meantime, please try and stay out of trouble."

"I want you to know that I'm finished." Pricilla braced herself against the car door as Max took the curve in the road that led toward the lodge a few miles an hour too fast.

"Finished with what?"

Rows of pine trees streaked by as gravel crunched beneath the tires. "I'm finished with my role of amateur sleuth. No more Miss Marple, Jessica Fletcher, or Sherlock Holmes."

Max shot her a wry look. "Does that mean I can't be your Dr. Watson anymore?"

"Stop teasing. I saw the way you looked at me in the sheriff's office."

"I was honestly madder at his tactics than yours. Neither of us could have predicted Stewart's explosion."

Pricilla gripped the door handle. "Can you slow down just a little bit, please?"

"I'm sorry." He let up on the gas. "My mind isn't exactly on the road at the moment."

"Neither is mine. I've presumably managed to get Annabelle's son arrested for murder."

Max reached out and squeezed her hand. "If he does end up getting arrested, you had nothing to do with it. The truth would have come out one way or another. And Stewart's the one who will have to pay the consequences."

"I suppose." She glanced down at Max's solid hand that enclosed hers. He always made her feel so safe and protected. "What I do know is that I'm finished with the whole sleuthing thing. I'm now simply Pricilla Crumb, chef at the Rendezvous Hunting Lodge and Resort."

"And girlfriend to Max Summers?"

She caught the gleam in his eye and felt a rush of adrenaline fill her heart. "Girlfriend sounds a bit. . . juvenile, don't you think?"

"Juvenile or not, with sleuthing out of the way, there might actually be time to give our relationship a go." He raised her hand to his lips and kissed her fingertips. "What do you think?"

That Max Summers was more romantic than Clark Gable and Cary Grant rolled into one sweet package?

She let out the breath she'd been holding. "I think that can be arranged."

"Good."

Outside they were surrounded by dozens of shimmering aspen trees, a colorful display of spring flowers, and the mighty Rocky Mountains, but all she could see at the moment was Max's handsome profile. He'd swept in unexpectedly and brought things into her life she'd forgotten were missing. Widowhood had left her longing for someone to hold her hand when she was lonely, someone to laugh with and cry with. Max was filling up the lonely spots.

Annabelle's lost expression flashed through the recesses of her mind. Her friend might not have had an ideal marriage with Reggie, but they'd still managed to stick together for all those years. Pricilla understood the pain of losing a husband. That's why the thought of loving then losing Max had her running scared at times. But even her sometimes irrational fears couldn't compare with what Annabelle was going through.

"I'm still worried about Annabelle. My gut tells me that Stewart wouldn't murder anyone. I just wish there was a way to prove it—"

"Pricilla—"

"Don't worry. I meant what I said about staying out of the investigation, but I still can't help but worry about Annabelle's family."

Max pulled into the driveway of the lodge and parked the car in an empty space. "All Annabelle needs at this point is a friend, and nothing more."

"I know. You're right."

He squeezed her hand one last time before opening his car door and letting in a gush of warm spring air. "Of course I'm right."

Chuckling, Pricilla made her way up to the porch where Nathan and Trisha sat in the afternoon sun, drinking lemonade and snacking on a plate of her double fudge brownies.

Pricilla noticed the bleak expressions that crossed the couple's faces and paused at the top of the stairs. "Surely my brownies aren't that bad."

"Of course not. They're the only appealing thing I see at the moment." Trisha folded her arms across her chest and shot Pricilla an exasperated look. "Nathan and I have just officially had our first fight."

"I'm shocked it took you this long." Max stopped behind Pricilla and laughed. "And if you're wondering if it will be your last, I can assure you that it won't."

Pricilla picked up Penelope from her padded perch on one of the chairs and sat down with the cat across from the couple. "Do I dare ask you what you fought about, or would that be sticking my nose into yet another subject that isn't my business?"

"It's not a secret at all." Nathan held up the hunters' calendar that normally hung above his desk in his office. "We're trying to set a date."

"For the wedding?" Pricilla didn't understand the problem.

Trisha shrugged. "Sounds petty, I know, but nailing down a date that will work for both of us is proving to be a tad difficult."

"A tad?" Nathan dropped the calendar onto an empty chair. "How about impossible?"

"Don't start it all again." Max grabbed a brownie from the plate then sat down, seemingly amused with the situation. "Why don't you simply hire one of those wedding planners who will make all the major decisions for you? If you can't set a date, how in the world will you choose colors, flowers, dresses, and all the other stuff that women insist on when it comes to planning a wedding?"

Pricilla frowned. "Are you trying to pick a fight with me now?"

Max winked at her. "Nothing of the sort. I was simply trying to help."

"That's not helping, Dad." Trisha waved her hands in the air. "And please don't even go there. This is my wedding, and I refuse to have the details handled by a stranger."

"It's *our* wedding," Nathan cut in.

"Of course it's our wedding, but—"

"Elope with the girl, Nathan." Max crossed his ankles, looking completely relaxed. "It's the only way to survive your upcoming nuptials."

"They wouldn't dare." Pricilla had held her tongue long enough. "They'd forever have the wrath of a mother who's been dreaming of her only son's wedding for over thirty years."

"Mother—"

"What? Is it asking too much to be a part of the wedding of my son and the woman he loves?" Pricilla grabbed a brownie, pulled a walnut off the top, then hesitated before sticking it into her mouth. "What's the problem with deciding on a date anyway? I would think that out of 365 days in a year you could agree on at least one date."

Trisha flicked her fingers against the calendar. "Hunting season."

"Hunting season is not the problem—"

"Of course it is, Nathan." Trisha rolled her eyes. "I have to plan my wedding around hunting season. And I've always wanted a fall wedding."

"Women are stubborn, Nathan." Max still looked as if he were enjoying the conflict. "You're going to have to get used to it."

"You're not helping, Dad."

Pricilla felt her blood pressure rising. She'd deal with Max later. Right now there was a wedding to rescue. "Trish is right, but what you should be thinking about is that the actual wedding is only one day out of your life together. I think you're both forgetting that what really counts is the marriage. Not the wedding. If you can't learn to give and take now, it's going to be rough."

Nathan raked his fingers through his hair. "I love Trisha, you all know that, but I've been a bachelor for so long—"

"And that makes you some sort of hero who deserves special treatment?" Pricilla frowned. The entire conversation was getting ridiculous. "Trisha left her home and moved to Colorado so the two of you could make a go of this relationship. Give and take is what will make your marriage work."

Pricilla stopped. Weren't Nathan's excuses the same excuses she'd been throwing out regarding her relationship with Max? She was too old to make another big change in her life. Too stuck in her ways to make the necessary adjustments that would give their relationship a chance. Max had made the first move in agreeing to stay in Rendezvous, and instead of being grateful she continued to push him away with her excuses.

Trisha clasped her hands in her lap. "Your mother's right, you know."

Nathan dropped the calendar to the floor. "That I'm being the stubborn one."

"I didn't say—"

"I know. I'm sorry." He reached out and wrapped his hands around Trisha's. "My mom is right. A relationship is all about give and take, but we've somehow gotten so caught up in this wedding planning stuff that we've forgotten what's really important."

"And what is that?"

"You and I living the rest of our lives together." Nathan leaned forward and kissed Trisha slowly on the lips. "I'm sorry."

A glow flickered once again in Trisha's eyes as she looked at him. "Me, too."

Nathan stood then pulled Trisha to her feet. "How about we go for a walk and figure out a compromise. The weather's perfect. . .you're perfect. . ."

She let out a soft giggle. "I think we can do that."

Taking Trisha's hand, Nathan led her toward the stairs. "We'll be back in a little bit."

Pricilla watched them walk across the lawn that was edged with yellow primroses and sweet violets, their arms around each other. "They make a sweet couple, don't they? There's something so romantic about being young and in love."

Max quirked an eyebrow. "Versus being old and in love."

"I didn't mean that at all." She caught his smile and tried to understand the countless emotions that filled her heart, knowing Max loved her. Joy mixed with fear and contentment. Perhaps she was making it all too complicated. "There's nothing like falling in love for the first time and promising the rest of your life to another person. I'd given up on ever having grandkids until now."

"You know we've got our own quandary to work out."

"I know, and I think I've figured out at least part of what's been bothering me." Pricilla swallowed hard. How was it that solving dilemmas between Trisha and

Nathan seemed so simple compared to her own life?

"Okay. What have you figured out?"

"Your moving here does change everything."

"In a bad way?"

"Of course not. In a different way." Pricilla stared out across the green grass as the silhouette of Nathan and Trisha disappeared into a grove of pine trees. "Listening to the two of them made me think. When you were in New Mexico, I didn't have to think seriously about where our relationship was going because of the distance between us. But now. . ."

"I'm here and you have to decide."

"Exactly." Pricilla nodded. At least he seemed to understand. "And it's not as if I don't want things to move forward between us, but this is scary for me, Max. I loved one man for forty-three years. Falling in love again is wonderful, beautiful, and exciting, but also very unexpected. And even a bit scary."

"I guess it boils down to one question, then." His gaze caught hers. "Do you want me to stay, Pricilla?"

16

Pricilla stepped into the fourth townhouse she and Max had looked at in the past two hours. All of their charming features, as the Realtor called them, were beginning to blur together. One bedroom versus two bedrooms. Wood fireplaces versus gas. An extra half bath versus an extra full bath. . . She glanced at the tacky gold curtains hanging above a large picture window. None of that really mattered. What really mattered was that Max was staying.

That *was* what mattered most. Wasn't it?

She studied him as he circled the living room, looking like a serious renter. Max, with his gorgeous blue eyes and handsome physique, was staying because of her. That very idea kept repeating in her mind over and over and made her heart pound with anticipation. It was what she wanted, of course, because with him living close by they would have a chance to see if their relationship really had a chance.

No.

Not *if* their relationship had a chance. It would allow what they already had to blossom and grow into marriage. Which was what they both wanted. Max would rent a small place for six months or so, and in the meantime they would spend time together like any other dating couple until he proposed.

Except if that were true, then why did she have to keep telling herself that this was what she wanted?

She ran her fingers across a dusty windowsill in the small living room and decided to focus on the matter at hand. House shopping. The view of the Rocky Mountains from the front window was stunning. A bit of spring cleaning and new curtains could easily transform the neglected dwelling into the perfect bachelor pad. If they married. . .once they married. . .there would be further logistics to work out, but those things didn't have to be decided at this point. All she needed to focus on now was that Max had decided to give up his life in New Mexico for her. And that he loved her.

Pricilla stayed in the background as Max chatted with the Realtor, Marilee Baxter, a middle-aged woman who sported tweezed eyebrows, fake finger-nails, and a wad of gum that seemed the essence of unprofessionalism. At least she had the decency to wear an outfit that covered up her lush curves, unlike some women prone to display all their assets in low-cut, tightly fitting attire.

"What is this for?" Max stared at one of the living room walls that had an indented arched space.

"It's called an art nook." Marilee moved in beside him, her hands waving along with her enthused explanation. "It's a charming place to feature a lovely antique vase, or—"

"I don't own any vases." Max frowned.

"If you don't have any vases, perhaps you could hang a small framed picture." Marilee brought her hand to her mouth and shuddered. "Of course, now any mention of a vase reminds me of Reggie Pierce.

You have heard the horrible news about poor old Reggie, Rendezvous' famed baker, haven't you?"

"Yes, I—"

Marilee didn't even pause for Max's reply. "Everyone in town's talking about how someone knocked him off with a heavy vase. Have you ever imagined such an awful way to die?" The woman finally paused to take a breath and snap her gum. "Haven't had this much excitement since Naomi Tucker, the town librarian, was found dead eleven years ago on the bank of Lake Paytah, wearing a purple scuba diving suit."

"I'm not sure that *excitement* is the right word." Max glanced in Pricilla's direction. "Pricilla actually was—"

Pricilla shook her head and moved to stand beside him. The last thing she needed was the entire town talking about how she had been the one to discover Reggie's body. Thanks to the detective, no doubt, her name had stayed out of the paper, a fact she would be eternally grateful for. Not only did the omission keep the lodge out of any connection to a second murder, she also had no desire to have her name aligned once again with such an awful event. Apparently Detective Carter was good for something after all.

One slipped word to Marilee, though, and Pricilla was quite certain that her involvement in yet a second murder investigation would become as legendary as the deceased town librarian.

"What about Pricilla?" Marilee spoke as if Pricilla were in the room and she was looking for the latest town gossip to spread through the fertile grapevine.

Pricilla decided to speak up for the first time. "Max was only saying that because I'm friends with Reggie's wife, Annabelle, and the news came as quite a shock to all of us."

Max flashed Pricilla an apologetic look. He'd have to get used to the small-town mentality where gossip spread faster than a wildfire and never came out the same story at the other end.

"Such a sad account." Marilee folded her arms across her chest. "I ate at Reggie's restaurant in New York years ago while in town for a conference."

"Really?" Pricilla couldn't help but ask the probing question. She might have promised to stop her investigation, but the fact that Reggie's partner from that very New York restaurant had mysteriously died before the place shut down wasn't a piece of information that she could simply forget. And while she couldn't see how it had any relevance to Reggie's death, she was curious about the place. "What was the restaurant like?"

Max glanced at his watch. "Perhaps we should continue the tour of this place. It is getting late—"

"I was quite impressed, actually." Marilee leaned against the stone fireplace, seemingly absorbed with the new topic. "It catered to a wealthier crowd and the food was sensational. You're a chef, aren't you, Mrs. Crumb?"

"Yes."

"You would have loved this place. It was tucked away at the end of a quiet street, but that didn't stop the crowds from coming. When I ate there, we waited an hour and a half for a table for four, and let me tell you, it was worth every minute. They had a chef straight from some fancy chef school in Paris who could turn out the most divine escargot, baked shallots, and the pasta. . .well, it was an experience I'll never forget."

To the woman's advantage, she had just set upon Pricilla's favorite topic. "You're making me hungry, and it's not even dinnertime yet."

"Just the savory smells alone, at this restaurant, would have packed on the calories." Marilee's smile faded. "There was something strange about their move here, though."

Pricilla took a step forward. "What was that?"

"Perhaps we could look at the kitchen—"

"I've always believed that Reggie must have had a stash of cash somewhere," Marilee continued, ignoring Max's comment. "The restaurant had a price-less collection of antiques displayed that was quite stunning. Things like rare porcelain pieces, turquoise corded vases, and a number of valuable prints. I've always had quite an eye for expensive antiques, so naturally, when the family moved here and I became their Realtor, I expected them to buy one of the more upscale accommodations Rendezvous has to offer. We have some spectacular pieces of property available, you know."

"Naturally."

Max might not be smiling along with his sarcastic comment, but Pricilla couldn't help but urge the woman to continue. "And why didn't they? Buy something more exclusive, I mean?"

"Frankly, I'm not sure. Their decision to move in above the bakery surprised me. Granted, not only is it convenient, but the accommodations are quite large and well built. But still. One would assume that they would have had the money to move into something a bit more luxurious." Marilee leaned forward and lowered her voice. "On the other hand, I have heard rumors that the reason they moved here was because the restaurant went belly-up. It's hard for me to imagine how, except for some sort of problem in the management, but nevertheless, it would be a shame to have had to sell all those beautiful pieces."

"Ladies, if you don't mind." Max stepped in between them. "While the subject of a dead man's antiques and hidden stash of money is fascinating, at the moment I'm more interested in finding a place that will hold *my* antiques. A cracked leather sofa, a worn plaid recliner, and half a dozen cheap, secondhand prints."

Marilee's eyes widened for a brief second before she gained back her composure. Undoubtedly, hearing the word *antique* anywhere near the words *cracked leather*, *worn plaid*, and *cheap* was turning her stomach sour.

Pricilla tried not to laugh as Marilee cleared her throat and addressed Max. "My apologies, Mr. Summers. You're completely correct in your statement that we need to get back to the business at hand. I don't know what got into me. Shall we hurry on to the kitchen then? You're going to absolutely love the charming bay window in the breakfast nook."

"I'm sure I will." Max brushed against Pricilla as Marilee sped toward the kitchen and stopped. "I thought Miss Marple had vanished from the picture."

"She has." Pricilla frowned. "Only she seems to have left behind her friend, Miss Curiosity, who simply can't be held accountable for asking a few innocent questions."

"Innocent?" He squeezed her arm and placed an unexpected kiss on her cheek. "You know you're incurable, Mrs. Crumb."

By the fifth house, Max was beginning to question his decision to leave New Mexico and rent a house. Not that he had changed his mind about being closer to Pricilla, but he did wish that there was another way. His place back home had a large storage shed for his tools and various woodworking hobbies. None of these houses had an area for him to tinker around on his latest project.

And there was another thing that was bothering him. Pricilla. Not that she'd said anything specifically, but he was quite certain that she still had doubts regarding their relationship.

Marilee's phone rang with some fast-paced rap song that sounded as loud and flamboyant as the woman herself. "If you will both excuse me for a moment."

With a nod of her head, she disappeared off onto the back porch that overlooked the mountains. The one *charming* asset of the place Max actually agreed with her on.

Pricilla stared out the window, her arms crossed

and her lips puckered into a frown.

Max moved to stand beside her. "Another beautiful view."

"True."

A one-word response from her could only mean one thing. "What's wrong, Pricilla?"

She spun toward him and forced a smile. "Nothing. I just. . .I suppose I'm just worried a bit that you really want to go through with this move. I mean, it is a rather big change."

"Do you want me to move closer?" While he was uncertain where their conversation was leading, he was afraid he wasn't going to like the final destination.

"Of course I want you nearby. I just don't want you to ever feel. . .obligated."

The tone of her voice was far from convincing. "Are you really sure you want me to stay, Pricilla?"

He brushed his fingers across her forearm. He hated to ask her a second time, but he couldn't ignore the flicker of doubt in her eyes that had seemed to grow with each house they'd stepped inside. He knew that his move to Colorado had been a rather impulsive one, and he had made it a priority to pray that they make the right decision, but something still wasn't right.

He stepped back to lean against the kitchen counter. "I need to know where you want our relationship to go."

Pricilla's eyes widened. "You know I want you to stay."

"Actually, I'm not convinced. And while I don't want to say good-bye. . ."

She turned back to the window, her silence speaking more than words ever could. "I know you've wanted me to be more decisive regarding our relationship, and I honestly don't know why I feel so confused."

"Does it have anything to do with Marty?"

"I loved Marty for over half my life, but this is more than losing him." Her fingers fumbled with the blue curtains hanging in the window. "Honestly, I don't think my reservations have anything to do with Marty, except for on one level, I suppose. Losing him hurt so much. . .I just don't want to go through it all again."

Max resisted reaching out and pulling her toward him. The last thing he wanted to do was completely push her away. "I understand what it's like to lose someone you love, but I'm sixty-five years old. I'm not getting any younger."

Max closed his eyes for a moment and prayed for the right words. He never had been good at discussing his feelings, but this moment, of all moments, he was going to have to make a gallant try.

Pricilla swung around to face him. "I don't know if I'm ready, Max."

"I—"

Marilee waltzed back into the kitchen and shoved her phone into her black bag. "So, where were we?"

"I'm sorry, but. . ." Max ignored the woman's bright expression and turned to Pricilla, who avoided his gaze. His heart sank like a downed missile. "I'm sorry, Marilee, but there's been a slight change of plans."

⁓

Pricilla didn't remember the last time she'd felt so completely guilt-ridden. Most likely not since she believed herself to have poisoned Mr. Woodruff with one of her salmon-filled tartlets. At least in that case she'd been absolved of the horrific deed, but in this instance, with Max's broken heart exposed beside her, there was no one to blame but herself.

She squeezed on the handle of the car door until her knuckles turned white. How could she have been such a fool and pushed Max away because of her own irrational fears? Staring out the window of the car, she watched the trees fly by as Max drove her back to the lodge. Life was full of loving and losing. Sixty-five years on this earth had been enough to teach her that. Even the Bible talked about times of laughter and tears, so why, as an individual who, more often than not, tended to jump into things without always fully analyzing the consequences, was she unable to give love a fair shot at happiness?

To give her and Max a fair shot at happiness.

She turned to catch a glimpse of him out of the corner of her eye. He gazed straight ahead, his expression harsher than normal. She knew she'd hurt him tremendously, but no matter how bad she felt, she couldn't find a way to erase the flood of doubts that continued to assault her.

He eased up on the accelerator before turning onto the road that led to the lodge. As soon as he dropped her off, he'd undoubtedly be on the next plane to New Mexico—miles away from the senseless woman who'd just managed to throw her heart away and stomp on his in the process.

She cleared her throat. "I'm sorry."

"You have nothing to be sorry about."

"I have everything to be sorry about. How can I, Ms. Spontaneity, suddenly freeze when it comes to matters of the heart?"

"It happens to the best of us." Max's tone was even, but the hurt in his voice was clear.

"So this has happened to you before?"

"Well. . .no." He continued to avoid her gaze. "I've only loved two women in my life."

Her and Violet. The guilt Pricilla felt deepened another notch. Violet had been his high school sweetheart before becoming his wife for forty or so years. Did the fact that she *did* love him count for anything at this point?

"I do love you, Max. I just need more time—"

"For what?" Gravel spun beneath the tires as Max took the left curve too sharply. "I've waited for months, and like it or not, I'm not going to be around forever. I was looking forward to sharing my twilight years with you while there was still something left to enjoy. One of these days, I'm going to start forgetting more than just where I laid my glasses or what I had for breakfast yesterday. I'm going to—"

"You're not that old."

"At the moment I'm not feeling that young, either."

Pricilla jumped as her cell phone went off in her purse. The interruption was only going to serve as a delay to the inevitable falling out that was coming between them, and the whole idea made her sick. Digging through the bag, she tried to squeeze out the tears that rimmed her eyes. She'd never meant for things to end this way between them.

"Hello?"

"Mrs. Crumb?" A tentative male voice responded on the other end.

"Yes. Who is this?"

"This is. . .Naldo. I work at the Baker's Dozen in Rendezvous." There was a slight pause on the line. "I'm not sure if you remember meeting me—"

"Of course I remember. Can I help you somehow?"

"I need to speak with you in person."

Pricilla mentally sorted through her calendar for the next couple of days. "I suppose I could drop by the bakery tomorrow—"

"I need to speak with you today, if at all possible."

She furrowed her brow, uncertain of the rationale behind the urgency in his voice. "Well, I suppose I could come today. What did you have in mind?"

"Not the bakery. There's a small Mexican restaurant twenty miles outside of Rendezvous in the town of Mountain Springs. Can you meet me there in half an hour?"

"Half an hour?" Pricilla glanced at her watch. "I don't know. I—"

"Please, Mrs. Crumb. It has to do with Mr. Pierce's death."

Pricilla sucked in a short breath. Max was not going to like this. She'd promised to give up her sleuthing. To forget about Sherlock Holmes and Jessica Fletcher. . .

"Mrs. Crumb, I think I know who killed him."

17

Pricilla snapped the cell phone shut and dropped it into her purse. If Naldo was telling the truth, then the odds of discovering who had killed Reggie had just risen a notch or two. The logical thing might be to call Carter and tell him what had happened, but she knew she needed to talk to Naldo first.

The problem was explaining it to Max.

"Who was that?" Max gripped the wheel.

"Naldo." Pricilla worked to keep her voice even. "He works for Annabelle at the Baker's Dozen. You met him the day we toured—"

"I remember." Max appeared not to catch the lighthearted mood she attempted to display. "Why would he call you?"

"He. . . Max, would you mind stopping the car for a moment?"

"Stop the car? Why?"

"Please?"

Frowning, Max dropped his speed and edged closer to the side of the road. "What's going on?"

Pricilla held up her hands. "Before I say anything else, please understand that I honestly had every intention of stepping out of the role of detective and leaving the case completely in Carter's hands. No more subtle interviews with suspects. No more notebooks full of motives. No more—"

"I get it, Pricilla." Max was not smiling.

"Just remember, when you start getting mad, that this wasn't my idea."

"What wasn't your idea?" A vein in his neck began to pulse. "What did Naldo want, Pricilla?"

"He thinks he knows who killed Reggie."

Max slammed on the brakes and came to a complete stop. "Pricilla!"

"Stop saying Pricilla like you're calling me to the principal's office to be expelled, or—"

"That's exactly what I'm trying to sound like." He shifted the car into PARK and took his hands off the steering wheel. "This is insane. You need to call Detective Carter right now and tell him about this meeting."

He grabbed for her purse, but she clutched it against her chest. "I don't think that's a good idea."

"Pricilla—"

"Max." She mimicked his patronizing tone.

"I'm sorry, but how in the world could calling the police *not* be a good idea?"

"If he wanted the police involved, don't you think Naldo would have called them up himself? He wants to talk to me. He's scared."

"Of what?"

"I don't know, but I could hear it in his voice."

"Face it, Pricilla. Your instincts about people haven't always been on target."

Now he was beginning to tread on thin ice. "I was right about Ezri having a secret, and Stewart—"

"Fine. Perhaps at times you at least hit the dart-board. . ." Max pounded his hands against the steering wheel. "But there's no way I'm taking you to meet this guy."

"Then I'll go on my own."

She jutted out her chin, annoyed at his negative response. She deserved a bit of credit. It wasn't as if she wanted to apprehend the murderer herself. All she wanted to do was see what Naldo wanted. Besides, how dangerous could it be to meet him at a public place?

Max shifted in his seat and faced her. "Can I ask you a question? Why is it that you're so decisive on this matter, yet falling in love and committing to a person is impossible for you?"

She tried to ignore the sting of his question but couldn't shake off its implications. "It's not impossible, and that wasn't a fair question."

"I'm sorry. You're right. That was a low blow."

"Yes, it was."

He stared at her for a moment as if he didn't know how to respond. "It's just that all the things I love about you are the very same things that get you into trouble and end up keeping us apart. I never know what you want."

"You don't know what I want?" Pricilla blinked back tears of frustration. "I want to erase every fear I have that is standing between you and me and a relationship. I want to let myself forget about the hurt and pain I felt when Marty died, and the knot in my gut that warns me not to go through it again with you. But for whatever reason, that hasn't happened yet. And until it does, it wouldn't be fair to either of us for me to commit to something I'm not completely sure about."

"I guess falling in love is complicated whether you're sixteen or sixty." For the first time, his expression softened, and he smiled at her.

"I guess you're right."

Max shifted the car into DRIVE and glanced into the rearview mirror before swinging a sharp U-turn in the gravel road. "If we're going to get there in time, we'd better get going."

⁓

Max followed Pricilla up the flower-lined sidewalk toward the entrance of the restaurant and wondered how he'd managed to once again give in to her. Granted, part of him was interested in what Annabelle's employee had to say, but common sense required them to go to the detective with the lead. Following up on this information themselves was apt to get them into all sorts of trouble. Though surely things couldn't get much worse than Pricilla's recent arrest and their both being hauled down to the sheriff's office.

That is, unless Naldo was the murderer and they were stepping into a trap.

Ignoring the ridiculous thought, Max opened the glass door of the restaurant and released the savory scents of spices and fresh chips into the afternoon air. His stomach growled, reminding him that lunch had been a long time ago. He loved Mexican food—or at least he had twenty years ago. Today spicy foods tended to leave him regretting the indulgence. Perhaps just one order of mild salsa or guacamole with a basket of tortilla chips wouldn't affect him that much.

Pricilla stopped just inside the doorway and turned to him. "Are you sure you're okay with this?"

He glanced inside the quiet restaurant where only a half dozen or so clients were left after the presumed lunch rush. Upbeat salsa music played in the background, far too peppy for his current mood. "It's a little too late to back out now, I suppose."

She shot him a half smile, and his heart lurched. This wasn't fair. Thirty minutes ago she'd managed to break his heart, yet here he stood beside her, hot on the trail of one of her suspects who'd promised them vital information. The way things had gone so far, they were more likely to be classified as criminals along with the likes of Bonnie and Clyde than end up as heroes by solving the case. What did it matter anyway? As soon as they were done here, he planned to drop Pricilla back off at the lodge and catch the next flight to New Mexico.

He turned away from her and took in the dining room that had been decorated in the southwestern flair common to most Mexican restaurants. He just wished her silver curls and hazel eyes hadn't left such a lasting imprint on his mind. He'd have to deal with his heart later. Right now it was up to him to make sure Pricilla didn't get herself into any trouble. Or manage to drag him into it with her.

Pricilla tugged at his sleeve. "I don't want you mad at me for agreeing to come out here. You know I never planned this."

Max couldn't help but laugh at her plea of innocence.

"As much as I hate to admit it, it does seem to me that intrigue has a way of finding you whether you want it or not."

"And speaking of intrigue." Pricilla pointed toward the other side of the room. "There he is. And he's alone."

Max nodded as a waitress dressed in a decorative, flared skirt and bright orange blouse approached them with a broad smile.

"Table for two?"

Pricilla shook her head. "Thank you, but we're meeting someone on the other side of the room."

Without another word, she scurried past the waitress and barely missed knocking into a six-foot-tall cactus displaying half a dozen sombreros.

Following her across the room, Max slid into the cracked leather seat beside her and greeted Naldo, who looked as if he'd rather be anywhere else but here at the moment. Perhaps Max wasn't the only one feeling as if this interview might be a mistake.

Naldo swirled his glass of ice water, letting the frozen liquid clink against the edges. "I'm glad you both showed up, but I. . .I'm not sure this was a good idea."

"What is it, Naldo?"

A bead of sweat covered his temple and dripped down the side of Naldo's face. He sopped it up with his napkin before looking up again. "I called you because I owe Mr. Pierce. And like I told you, Mr. Summers, he and his wife have always been good to me."

Pricilla glanced up at Max, but he avoided her gaze. With all that had happened lately, the last thing he wanted to confess to was that he'd tried to do his own investigating.

"Someone's going to get into trouble." Naldo glanced at the exit then leaned forward. "And I have no intentions of being connected to a murder I didn't commit."

～

Pricilla shivered at the man's words. The word *murder* was enough to make her wish she'd taken Max's advice and forgotten about the whole investigation.

She decided to proceed cautiously. "You said you knew who was responsible for Reggie's death."

"I don't know for sure, but I do know that something odd is going on around that house, and I don't like it." The waiter placed a basket of chips and salsa on the table and Naldo looked relieved over the distraction. He dunked a crisp chip into the salsa. "Mr. Pierce might not have been the nicest man in the world with his temper and all, but he did give me and my brother a chance."

Pricilla eyed the salsa with interest but was quite certain it would be too hot for her taste. More than likely, she was already going to be up half the night, tossing and turning over her fumbled relationship with Max. There was no use adding heartburn to the mix.

"What makes you think something's going on at the Pierce home?"

Naldo took another chip. "First, you need to know that the only reason I'm telling you this is because you both seem like nice people. And when you dropped by the bakery, Mr. Summers, and tried to find out why I was rummaging through the trash. . .well. . .I realized later that I should have told you the truth then."

"You were interviewing suspects?" Pricilla stared at Max.

"It was nothing." Max grabbed a chip and stuffed it in his mouth.

"Nothing?" she pressed.

"Mrs. Crumb?"

Pricilla wavered before turning back to Naldo. She and Max could talk later.

"All I'm going to do is pass on what I know about Mr. Pierce's death. What you do with this information is your business, but don't expect me to go to the police and repeat any of this."

"Okay." Pricilla took a chip from the basket, ready for him to get to the point.

"But first of all, I want to make a deal."

"A deal?" What she needed was information that would be worthwhile to her. . .and to Carter. "I'm not sure what you mean. Could you explain?"

Naldo's gaze shifted to the table. "My brother and I are in the country illegally, and. . .well, with the detective snooping around in his investigation of Mr. Pierce's death, we're getting a bit nervous. I have a family to support back in Mexico. I need this job."

"I'm sorry, but I don't know anything about immigration laws or. . ." Pricilla shook her head and looked to Max.

"Neither Pricilla nor I can make any promises, Naldo." Max spoke up for the first time. "You have to understand that."

"But you can try. Can't you?"

"Why don't we start by you telling us what you

know. Then we can go from there."

Naldo scooted back in his chair, and for a moment she was afraid he wasn't going to trust them enough to continue. "I guess I could do that—"

"Are you all ready to order?"

The waitress took the most inopportune time to interrupt. From the way Naldo sat squirming in his chair, Pricilla was certain it wouldn't take much for the man to bolt.

"Why don't you order yourself something to eat if you're hungry," Max told him. "I'll pick up the bill."

Pricilla felt a wave of gratefulness wash over her at Max's offer. Dr. Watson, it seemed, had returned.

"I don't know." Naldo stared at the menu.

Pricilla felt her blood pressure rise a notch. While she did appreciate Max's offer and felt certain that a serving of good food would help put Naldo at ease, waiting on the dark-haired man to tell them what he knew left her with the same feeling she'd had the summer Nathan talked her into bungee jumping off the edge of a bridge.

Thirty long seconds later, Naldo set the menu back on the table. "I'll take a plate of enchiladas rancheras with a side of guacamole."

"Pricilla?" Max seemed anything but anxious.

"Thanks, but I'm really not hungry." Food was the last thing she wanted when a bomb was about to explode in her lap. "But I will take a lemonade, please."

The young woman scribbled something on her pad before turning to Max. "And you, sir?"

"Make that two sides of guacamole, and a bowl of your tortilla soup would be great." Max folded his hands in front of him as the waitress left with their order. "The food smells wonderful here."

"It's the best in the area. My brother and I come here whenever we can."

Pricilla was not in the mood for casual, beat-around-the-bush conversation. "I believe Naldo was getting ready to tell us what he knew regarding the death of Reggie."

"Okay." Naldo rolled his napkin between his fingers. "Three times now I've seen Darren Robinson sneak into the Pierces' upstairs home."

"So that's why you were going through his trash?" Max asked.

"His trash?" Pricilla caught the flicker of guilt in Max's gaze.

Max waved his hand. "It was nothing."

"Thought I might be able to find something. . ." Naldo began.

"We can talk about the trash later. What I want to know is, why would Darren sneak into the Pierces' home?" Pricilla's eyebrows rose.

Naldo dunked another chip in the salsa before taking a bite. "I've been asking myself the same question. Last night I decided to follow him."

Pricilla leaned forward, not wanting to miss a single word. "And. . ."

"He had a key to the front door. Walked in like he owned the place."

"Where were Annabelle and Stewart?"

Max pressed his hands against the tabletop. "If you'd stop interrupting, he'll have a chance to tell us."

"Sorry." Pricilla stifled a grin. While he might never admit it, Max was as anxious as she was to get the truth out of Naldo.

"It was about two-thirty, so they were presumably in bed. I stood near the doorway, careful to stay in the shadows, and I saw Darren pull some papers out of the bottom shelf of the living room bookshelf. The only light in the room was from the full moon, but it was enough to tell me that he was happy. I think he found whatever it was he was after."

Pricilla leaned forward. "Which was. . . ?"

Naldo shrugged. "I never found out, because at that moment someone flipped on a light in the kitchen. It was a miracle neither of us was caught. I am, though, convinced about one thing. Darren found whatever it was he was looking for in the bookcase and would have taken it if someone hadn't scared him away. He managed to sneak out the door while I hid and slipped out a few minutes later. He's been looking for something, and I'm positive he'll be back."

Back at the lodge an hour later, Pricilla sat at the kitchen table and mulled over what Naldo had told them then pondered what Marilee had mentioned regarding her firsthand view of Reggie's New York restaurant. Was there a connection between the stash of money and Reggie's recent death? But how was Darren involved in all of this?

Somehow, on the way home, she'd convinced Max to stay another day, though he refused to discuss the case with her. Or the fact that he'd done a bit of his own investigating without telling her. Not that she had anything at this point either, but if she could find out if Reggie had something worth being killed for. . .

With Max dozing on the front porch of the lodge, Pricilla fired up the laptop. With what Darren taught her about the Internet, it was possible that she could find a connection between the young man and Reggie's past. If not, she had no proof that what Naldo had told her was even true.

All they really had at this point was Naldo's word. There was no proof yet that Darren really was after anything, or that Naldo hadn't made up the entire story. It was hardly enough information to take to the detective, something Pricilla was secretly glad for. She needed time to figure things out, and going to the sheriff would only mean that things were once again out of her hands. For the moment, she'd been given another opportunity to find out the truth. And if she could find a connection between Darren and Reggie she'd be one step ahead.

She began scanning page after page of newspaper clippings on the famed New York restaurant owned by Reggie and his partner, William Roberts. Every review promised that the restaurant would be around for years to come. But something had gone wrong.

She flipped to the next screen then stopped. A photo on the previous page had looked familiar. Pricilla clicked the back arrow and stared at the photo of William Roberts. . .and his son. It was a snapshot that had been displayed at William's funeral. Her heart thudded inside her chest. He wore glasses now and his hair was longer, but there was no doubt about it. She'd finally found her connection. Darren Robinson's real name was Darren Roberts. And he was the son of Reggie's dead business partner.

18

For a full thirty seconds, Pricilla couldn't move. She stared at the slightly blurred photo and decided she had to be imagining things. Why in the world would Darren have changed his name then applied for a job with his father's old business partner? None of it made sense, especially the fact that Annabelle had never mentioned who Darren was.

Unless Annabelle didn't know.

Pricilla searched her memory for what she'd learned up to this point about Reggie's former business partner, William Roberts. He had a son who would have been about Darren's age. Darren had told her that he had attended boarding school and had rarely seen his father. Was it possible, too, that Reggie and Annabelle hadn't known the boy? Annabelle had mentioned the fact that she hadn't seen William's wife since before William's funeral. . . . Which meant that Darren could have shown up without them knowing who he was.

She gnawed on the end of her thumbnail. Up to this point, she'd failed to come up with a single motive for Reggie's death under Darren's name in her notebook. Now, in a matter of two hours, his motivation had just shot him to the top of her list.

Pulling out her notebook, she glanced through her scribbled handwriting, trying to tie everything together. Annabelle had once told her that Reggie had always insisted on investing diversely. What if the two business partners had invested in something together besides the antiques the Realtor had mentioned? Something that only the two of them knew about.

Something worth killing for.

She tapped her pen against the table and hoped she was looking in the right direction. Things that could be hidden in a house might range from rare coins to government bonds to jewels. And any of those things could have given Reggie motivation for killing his partner. But the scenario obviously didn't end there. Darren must have found out about his father's investments with Reggie. Investments that Reggie somehow had managed to keep for himself at his partner's death. Pricilla shivered at the two chilling speculations she was left with. Darren took a job at the bakery with the intention of not only finding revenge in killing Reggie, but in getting his hands on a fortune as well.

The problem now was proving her theory.

"What are you working on?"

Pricilla jumped and smacked her leg against the underside of the table. "Ouch."

"Sorry." Max slid into the chair beside her. "I didn't mean to startle you."

Blue eyes stared back at her, but instead of the warmth they normally held, she couldn't miss the reservation in his gaze. She rubbed the top of her knee to ease the throb that was going to leave a nasty bruise. "I'm fine, really."

For a moment, a deafening silence hung between them.

"Can I get you something to drink?" Pricilla jumped up from the table and, once at the counter, began digging through the tray of tea bags. "I know I'd like some tea right now, though I suppose I'd better stick to one without caffeine. You know how too much caffeine makes me jittery and—"

"You're rambling, Pricilla."

"I'm sorry." She'd never felt uncomfortable around Max. . .until now. What if, because of her insane accomplishment of turning him down, she'd ruined their friendship? That was something she couldn't deal with at the moment. She grabbed two of the tea bags then shoved the box back in its rightful place on the counter. "Did you have a nice nap?"

Max tapped his fingers against the table, apparently as uncomfortable as she was. "It was just a short catnap, but I do feel energized."

She grabbed the kettle and began filling it with water. "Why do you suppose they call short naps catnaps? I mean, a short nap for Penelope could be an hour or two—"

"Pricilla, I came in here to tell you something."

She pulled two mugs out of the cupboard then turned to catch his somber expression. Whatever it was, this wasn't going to be good. "What's wrong?"

"I booked a ticket for New Mexico a few minutes ago with the airline. I'm leaving in the morning."

Pricilla felt the air rush out of her lungs. While the news might be expected, it didn't take away the reality that Max's leaving was going to break her heart. No, that was ridiculous. She'd been the one to drive him away. How had their relationship managed to take more twists and turns than a good cozy mystery novel? "You don't have to go—"

His jawline tightened. "I do, and you know it."

"If I had more time—"

"Stop feeling guilty, Pricilla. I know we can't always control how we feel, and this just happens to be a case when one party's feelings are stronger than the other's. It's not your fault."

His words sounded more like they were coming from a defense lawyer standing in front of a judge rather than the jilted party of a relationship gone sour. But despite their softness, the words did nothing to ease the sting of guilt that was welling up around the edges of her heart like an allergic reaction. All of this was her fault. There was no way around it. Surely there was some sort of in-between relationship they could muster to keep.

She poured the hot water over the tea bags then carried the two mugs to the table. "What happens now, then? You leave and I never see you again?"

"Not hardly, considering our children are soon to be married. Besides, it's not as if we have to avoid each other. We'll always be friends, Pricilla." He reached out as if to touch her hand, out of habit perhaps, but then drew it back quickly. "Nothing can change that."

Except she already had changed everything between them. As unintentional and unplanned as her actions had been, she knew she'd have to live with the consequences of losing the second man—and probably the last man—who'd really loved her. Unconditionally with no reservations.

She'd been a fool to let him go.

Max stared at the computer screen and wondered if he'd wake up one day and realize what a fool he'd been for not fighting longer and harder for Pricilla. Except he had tried to stay and fight. She'd made it clear that she didn't want their relationship to go past the boundaries of friendship, and he had to accept that.

But what if they lost their friendship as well?

He took a sip of his tea and winced as the hot drink scalded his tongue. He hated the awkwardness that had wedged a gap between them deeper than all the miles between here and New Mexico ever could have. The laptop's screen saver, a serene rippling brook, splashed across the monitor. Another reminder that all his efforts had been in vain. So much for his brilliant idea to bring them closer together through modern technology. So much for his idea to start courting at sixty-five.

He needed to change the subject. "Who was that in the picture?"

Pricilla set down a mug of tea in front of him and perched on the edge of the chair beside him, ready to run, he supposed, if he said anything out of place. "Did the boy remind you of anyone you know?"

Max turned the screen toward him slightly and moved the mouse to turn off the screen saver. "Not that I can think of."

"Look again."

This time he lowered his bifocals. "I suppose. . .he does look a bit like Darren Robin—"

"Exactly."

Max shrugged, not getting her point. "And there's significance to this?"

"Considering that it's a picture taken with him and his father, William Roberts, yes. I'd say there's quite a bit of significance involved."

Max mentally rolled his eyes while frowning. So she was off on another red herring chase. When would she learn to trust the detective enough to leave all matters of a murder investigation to him? Perhaps their unexpected breakup had been for the best. It was obvious that she wasn't relinquishing her role as Jessica Fletcher despite the detective's constant verbal warnings and, even more appalling, her recent arrest.

He turned back to his tea and stared down at the dark liquid. "I don't see how it can be the Darren we know. Robinson and Roberts—"

"Darren could have changed his name."

He looked up, catching her gaze. "That doesn't make him a killer."

"Not that information alone, but who did Naldo see snooping around the Pierces' home? Darren Robinson." Pricilla dumped another spoonful of sugar into her tea as her voice rose a notch. "Darren knows something about what his father and Reggie invested in, and I believe he's after it."

He bit the inside of his lip. He hated the fact that she was beginning to make sense. "Pricilla—"

"Think about it, Max. Even you can't deny the fact

that I've stumbled upon—"

"Stumbled upon?" His eyes widened at her innocent plea. He might be able to admit that her line of reasoning had possible merit, but he had to draw the line somewhere. She'd found a minuscule crack in the door and had shoved it wide open.

"I didn't call Naldo. He called me, and then—"

"And then you managed to keep that information from Detective Carter while you continued sleuthing on your own."

Max shoved his tea aside and shook his head. Whether or not she had "stumbled" upon the information really wasn't the issue here. He should have driven her directly to the sheriff's office instead of agreeing to the meeting with Naldo. Things were quickly spiraling out of control, and the fact remained that this was a murder investigation—something they both seemed to keep forgetting—not a mystery dinner party with eight guests, a box of clues, and a phony victim.

A man was dead, and there was a murderer on the loose.

"Max?"

He avoided her pleading expression, along with those eyes that always managed to pierce straight through his heart, and held up his hands in defeat. "All right. I'll admit that this is all information worth considering, but you've got to tell the detective what you've discovered."

"I will, but I want to try something first."

That wasn't a good sign. "Pricilla—"

"What's going on, you two?"

Max glanced up at the sound of Nathan's baritone voice as he and Trish entered the kitchen, hand in hand. At least they'd managed to salvage their relationship, unlike his own failed attempts with Pricilla.

"You have perfect timing." Pricilla jumped up from the table and grabbed two more mugs out of the cupboard. "I need to talk to all three of you about something. Sit down, and I'll pour you both a cup of tea."

"What it is, Mom?"

Max caught the questioning look Trish shot at Nathan as they sat down at the table. Pricilla had a plan, and he was quite certain that her plot was going to not only involve the three of them, but would undoubtedly transform them from respectable citizens into fugitives running from the wrath of Detective Carter. He wasn't sure he was ready this time. Even thirty-five years in the military hadn't prepared him for one of Pricilla's attempts to bring justice back into the world on her terms.

Pricilla set the two mugs in front of their children then slid into her chair while Max waited for the bomb to drop. "I know I promised that I was finished with the investigation of Reggie's death, and I was, scout's honor. But something. . .well, to put it bluntly, I think I know how to catch the killer."

Pricilla waited for a response, but no one said a thing. Instead, blank looks registered on their faces. Max looked as if he preferred to hide beneath the table rather than listen to her latest half-baked, concocted plan, as he was sure to think of it.

Obviously the blunt approach had not been a good choice.

"Max can back me up here." She cleared her throat. She had to make at least one valiant effort before they locked her away on some funny farm. "We think we know who killed him, which means—"

"*We* think we know?"

Pricilla decided to ignore the sting of Max's words. Perhaps switching to the plural to encompass him in her exploits hadn't been the wisest move, but this was going to take every bit of convincing she could muster. Giving herself the greatest advantage was simply good strategy on her part.

Pricilla took another sip of her tea, then, as succinctly and concisely as she could, she recapped the events of the last three hours, starting with the meeting with Naldo and ending with her discovery of Darren's true identity on the Internet. By the time she was finished, their blank looks had been replaced with a hint of interest. Perhaps only a small dose, but she was certain it was there nevertheless.

She leaned forward in her chair. "What do you think?"

"That you need to contact the detective immediately." There was no hesitation in Nathan's voice, a fact Pricilla chose to ignore as she continued.

"So you think my theory has merit?"

"Does that really matter in this instance?" There was no budging her son's stance.

It seemed as if in his eyes, her pursuit of justice

should have ended the moment it started. Never mind the fact that Annabelle was likely to go on trial for the murder of her husband, which in turn would affect her children and Kent. . . She felt a knot grow in her stomach. Not that she wanted to believe Darren had a role in Reggie's demise. She had found the young man polite and respectable, hardly the typical stereotype for a murderer. But then was there ever really such a thing? Murderers all had their own character traits, and besides that, facts couldn't be altered like a size twelve pair of pants.

Pricilla took a deep breath and decided to stand by her convictions. "I think it does matter, Nathan."

"As much as I don't want to admit it, I think your theory does have merit." Trisha held her tea mug between both hands and avoided Nathan's sharp look. "But that doesn't change the fact that Nathan is right. The detective needs to be updated on all of this, because frankly this isn't your business. I mean, this is a murder investigation, and just because you once happened to shake down a murderer in a similar situation doesn't mean you need to try it again. You got lucky once. That's not liable to happen a second time."

"Maybe not, but I need you all to hear me out." There was no way she was giving up now. They might not understand her motivation, but fear would not be the thing that stopped her. "Annabelle's future is at stake here, and I promised her that I would do everything I could—"

"Your promise doesn't include risking your life, Mom."

Pricilla wished she could find a way to make her

son understand. "My plan is foolproof and safe."

"How can a plan to catch a murderer ever be foolproof and safe?" Trish's brow lowered. The young woman was crossing over to the skeptics' side.

"Look at the facts with me for just a moment." Pricilla was ready to throw out everything she had left. "Naldo saw Darren looking for something in Annabelle's home. We know that whatever he's after, the young man's determined, and after last night's interruption, I have no doubt that he'll be back. More than likely tonight, which means we don't have a lot of time to play around with. Tomorrow he could be gone, along with Reggie's fortune."

"This is all speculation, Mom. So you catch him for breaking and entering." Nathan smacked his hands against the table and shrugged. "You still haven't caught him for murder. Besides that, the kid's smart. If he smells something fishy, he'll be out of there in a heartbeat."

"And how can you be so sure that Annabelle doesn't know about whatever he's looking for?" Max spoke up for the first time. "Maybe she's already liquefied the assets and there's nothing left to find. He could be on a wild goose chase, as well."

"Naldo was convinced Darren found what he was looking for. He wasn't able to take it with him last night, which means he'll be back."

"So how do we catch him?"

"Trish." Nathan nudged her with his elbow.

"I'm glad you asked." Pricilla smiled, feeling the rush of impending victory in the air. "We're going to set a trap."

19

Max sat down in the metal office chair across from Detective Carter's desk, feeling better than he had all day. The three of them hadn't been able to talk Pricilla out of her crazy plan to catch Darren red-handed, but now she sat beside him ready to face the detective, who, he was quite certain, would put a stop to this crazy proposed plot of hers. Watching the detective's lips pucker into a scowl as he slid into his chair convinced Max further that it was inconceivable the detective would allow Pricilla to go ahead with her plan to set up Darren no matter how many times she said it was foolproof.

Catching a murderer was never foolproof, and if he couldn't persuade her of that fact, at least Carter could lay down the law or even threaten arrest, if necessary, to curb her insane plot.

"So, Mrs. Crumb, I understand you have some information for me?" The detective shoved his glasses up the bridge of his nose then steepled his hands in front of him.

Smug with a touch of arrogance. . . For the first time since Max had met the detective he was beginning to like the man, if only because he was the one man who could literally put a stop to Pricilla's plans.

Pricilla perched on the edge of her chair, her bulky purse in her lap. "I did discover something quite interesting today, Detective, though I do hope I'm not wasting your time, bringing you information you already have."

The detective pulled a notebook and pen from his shirt pocket. "As long as you haven't run off with a stolen ATV or been involved in another barroom brawl, I suppose I can give you a few moments of my time."

Pricilla squirmed in her chair. Max smiled. Perfect! In five minutes she'd have shared her information along with her crazy plan, and Carter would respond by having them both thrown out of his office.

As expected, Pricilla started with the phone call from Naldo. The detective's eyes widened through parts of the monologue as his pen took rapid notes, but other than a few grunts, he said nothing. Max listened to Pricilla's description of Darren that made him sound more like a member of the Italian mafia rather than a college-age computer geek. That, though, was fine. The further offtrack she got, the quicker the detective would put an end to this.

Three minutes later Pricilla leaned forward for her closing argument. "So as you can see, the evidence all points to Darren, Detective. He got a job at the bakery not only to get his hands on Reggie's fortune, but to avenge his father's death."

Carter tapped his pen against the blotter on his desk. "Is that everything, Mrs. Crumb?"

"Isn't that enough?"

The detective stared at his handwritten notes then flipped a couple pages as he murmured something incoherent under his breath. "I have to admit that even though this information is coming from an amateur sleuth right out of the pages of an Agatha Christie novel, I think you might have something here."

"You do?" Max spoke up before he could stop himself.

Surely Detective Carter wasn't going along with Pricilla's line of reasoning? Granted, her ideas might warrant a second look at Darren's past involvement with the Pierce family and any connection he might have today, but the detective actually sounded. . . impressed.

Pricilla shot Max a victorious glance then cleared her throat. "Detective, I know you don't like the fact that I've interfered with your investigation a time or two in the past, but I have come up with a solid plan."

"A plan?"

"To trap Darren, of course." She held up her hand. "Before you stop me, please hear me out."

"Okay." Carter leaned back in his chair and folded his arms across his chest. "What do you propose to do?"

What did she propose to do?

Admitting that the information she'd come up with was helpful was one thing, but surely Carter wasn't open to listening to her harebrained scheme. Just because she'd been the one to put an end to their relationship didn't mean he wouldn't continue to be concerned over her wellbeing. He didn't want her involved.

". . .time is running out, and there's not a doubt in my mind, Detective, that Darren will be back tonight for what he left behind at the Pierce residence."

Detective Carter nodded his head. "I like it."

He liked it.

Liked what? Max frowned at the smile that passed between Pricilla and the detective. In his attempts to figure out the detective's motivations, he'd missed the crux of their conversation. And something else was bothering him as well. Since when did Pricilla and Detective Carter smile when in the same room together?

Max squirmed in his chair, shedding his confidence faster than a New Mexico rattlesnake could shed its skin. Had Carter really done the unthinkable and agreed to Pricilla's far-fetched plan? Max had only agreed to come with Pricilla because he knew the detective would put her in her place. And now the man was going along with her idea?

Impossible.

"I'll write a ransom note."

Max jerked his head up at the detective's statement. A ransom note hadn't been a part of Pricilla's plan. "You're going to do what, Detective?"

"Why not?" The lawman shoved his pen and notebook into his pocket and stood.

"It'll work." Pricilla's smile had yet to lessen.

Max shook his head. "I'm sorry, but I'm lost. I thought this entire plot was about arresting Darren."

"It is." Carter braced his hands against the top of the desk. "Haven't you been listening to a thing we've been talking about?"

"I. . ." How had he become the bad guy in this scenario? "Apparently I missed something."

"It's quite simple, really." Pricilla clutched her purse against her chest and stood up. "Looks as if you have a ransom note to write, Detective Carter."

Max frowned in defeat. None of this really mattered to him anyway. Pricilla could go through with her plan and there would be nothing he could do to stop her. He was leaving in the morning for New Mexico.

Two hours later Pricilla stood in the center of Annabelle's living room and faced a windowless wall, trying to ignore the sting of Max's hasty good-bye in the sheriff's parking lot. Not only had she managed to fumble their relationship, she'd apparently shot a hole in their friendship and sunk it as well.

Instead of sulking, though, she forced herself to refocus on the three six-foot-tall cherry bookshelves that stood side by side, encasing half a dozen shelves each. Reggie and Annabelle's collection of books was extensive, from classics like Twain and Dickens to bestselling authors King and Sparks to numerous nonfiction topics and business-related research material. If her theory was correct—and Naldo had been telling the truth—a fortune lay five feet away from her, hidden somewhere inside a secret compartment in the wooden frame.

"Pricilla?"

Pricilla spun around to face Annabelle, whose face had turned as pale as chalk since Pricilla's arrival thirty minutes ago. "I know you're nervous about all of this, but don't worry. It's going to work out fine."

Annabelle wrung her hands together in front of her. "What if it doesn't work?"

"We won't know unless we try, will we?" Pricilla moved across the oriental rug and squeezed her friend's hand. "It's all going to be over soon."

"I know." Annabelle blew her nose with a tissue from her pocket. "I sent Darren on an errand into Mountain Springs. He won't be back for at least another hour."

"Perfect. That will give us the time we need to make the exchange." Pricilla took a deep breath. No matter how knotted her nerves felt at the moment over the situation she'd gotten herself into, she was going to have to be the calm one. "Do you want to help with the search, or would you rather wait in my car?"

"Definitely wait in the car." Annabelle reached for her overnight bag and slung it over her shoulder. "Whatever Darren is after is the reason Reggie is dead, and part of me doesn't even want to know what it is. I still don't know how Reggie could have done this to me."

Pricilla pulled her friend into a hug. "I'm sorry, sweetie. I really am."

Tears welled up in Annabelle's eyes as she took a step back. "I thought I knew Reggie, but I didn't. I didn't know him at all."

"You go on downstairs while I wait for the detective." Pricilla worked to keep her voice even. "We shouldn't be too long."

Annabelle grabbed a black sweater off the back of the couch and headed for the front door. "I do appreciate your letting us stay at the lodge tonight. You've done so much for me. Too much."

"Nonsense. Once Darren finds out that Reggie's fortune has been switched for a ransom note, he's going to be furious. You don't want to be around to see those fireworks explode."

"Mrs. Crumb." Carter appeared in the doorway.

"Detective Carter. Good. You're back."

He shoved his hands into his front pocket and leaned against the doorframe. "Are you ready to go treasure hunting?"

Pricilla shot him a piercing stare. "Someone might hear you."

"Don't worry." The detective held up his hand. "With the investigation still open, no one will question my presence here. It's a small town, but even the news in Rendezvous can't get around that fast, so relax."

"Relax? Right." Annabelle slipped out the door, leaving Pricilla alone with the detective.

"Well, Mrs. Crumb." Carter rubbed his hands together like a kid ready for Christmas. She'd never seen him so. . .so enthusiastic about anything. "It all comes down to this. You find me a million-dollar stash, and I'll take your evidence to the DA. If we find nothing. . .well. . .then you're out of the game."

That sounded more like the detective she knew, and she couldn't help but wonder if he was more excited about finding Reggie's cache or proving her theory wrong. "Nothing like a bit of pressure."

"Now." Carter rested his hands on his hips. "Where exactly did Naldo say Darren had been when he stumbled across something?"

Pricilla walked across the room, stopping in front of the bookshelf. "Right about here."

"Then let's start looking."

Pricilla kicked the baseboard with the toe of her shoe, trying to feel for a slight give in the wood. Anything that might lead them to the alleged fortune Reggie had managed to squirrel away. "So why did you agree to my plan, anyway?"

She moved an inch to the left and jabbed at the board again.

Nothing.

Carter studied the bookshelf beside her. "Now that's a question I've asked myself at least a dozen times in the past two hours."

"Your confidence in me is overwhelming, Detective." Pricilla winced as she eased down on her hands and knees onto the wooden flooring. The last time she'd been in this position had been out of necessity when she spilled a bottle of Madge's expensive herbal supplements across her friend's linoleum kitchen floor. Still, she supposed that the chance of a vast fortune that would set Annabelle and her family up for life was reason enough to succumb to the aches and pains of growing old.

"Anything?" Carter crouched down beside her and ran his fingers across the next piece of baseboard.

"Not yet."

He blew out a deep breath then knocked against the wood. "You're sure Naldo was talking about these bookshelves—"

"Yes. He mentioned the bottom shelf."

"What if he meant floorboards, or—"

"Then why don't you bring him in for questioning?" Pricilla frowned. Just when she thought they'd managed to raise their relationship to the level of tolerance, he had to go and start being difficult again.

"I don't want to bring him in for questioning because we are trying to keep this treasure-hunting business under wraps, remember?" Carter stood and whacked the baseboard with the heel of his shoe. "If Naldo gets wind that the stakes might include a fortune, we'll have this house crawling with treasure hunters before I can count from *uno* to *diez*."

"Fine. Then keep looking."

Pricilla frowned. If they didn't find something soon, her entire theory would be shredded and thrown out with tomorrow's trash. If Naldo had been lying—

"Ouch!"

"Mrs. Crumb. What is it?"

"I just pinched my finger on something." Pricilla shook her finger, hoping to ease the stinging pain. "Wait a minute."

Without another thought to her injured finger, she began pulling the books off the bottom shelf. Two dozen encyclopedias might just be hiding more than an armload of interesting facts. With all the books tossed on the floor, she worked to lift up the bottom shelf.

"Look at this. You didn't have to take out all these books." Carter pulled a pocketknife from his pocket and pried at the bottom baseboard. A six-inch section popped off with a snap.

Pricilla picked up the piece of wood. "What is it?"

Carter motioned toward the small opening. "I suppose you deserve the honors."

Pricilla reached in her hand and pulled out a small black pouch. Diamonds scattered across the wood surface.

Carter started counting. "There's. . ."

"Thirteen."

He sat back on an encyclopedia before shoving it aside. "How appropriate."

"They're beautiful." Pricilla dropped one of the diamonds into the palm of her hand. "How much do you think these are worth?"

"I don't know." Carter held up one of the jewels toward the light. "They'll have to be appraised, of course, but I've heard of high-quality ones that ran for nearly half a million."

"Each?" Pricilla barely got the word out.

"Each."

Pricilla let out a low whistle. "So now we know what Darren was after."

"And what he was willing to kill for."

The next day, Pricilla filled the Styrofoam cup with steaming coffee then glanced around the newly opened convenience store at the edge of town. At nine o'clock the early morning traffic had dissipated, leaving the place quiet except for an old John Denver song that played over the sound system. While she would have preferred something more upbeat to counter her mood, the convenience store owner's choice in music was hardly at the top of her list of priorities. The detective had insisted that the setup here would be perfect in case something went wrong. Something she was praying wouldn't happen.

In the thirty minutes she had been here, she'd roamed the five aisles, counted the number of brands of cough drops, chips, and snack products, and rearranged a stack of crackers that had slid off the shelf. Perhaps her plan hadn't been so brilliant after all. It was a quarter past nine and there was no sign of Darren. He'd probably smelled a trap and run.

What had she been thinking? What had the detective been thinking when he set up this crazy scenario?

She wandered past the selection of drinks in the cooler section that ran along the back wall. Either the cashier was starting to get suspicious that she was stalking the place, or the young man was in on the operation with the detective. Carter had told her not to worry. Right. She'd give Darren another ten minutes before declaring defeat and trying to come up with plan B.

"Mrs. Crumb?" One of the cooler doors shut behind her. She turned around to face Darren. "What are you doing here?"

The boyish gleam she'd once recognized in his eyes had been replaced by a look of irritation. She opened her mouth to say something, but no words came out. She tried clearing her throat. High school students froze during the opening night of their senior play. The stakes here were much higher than a leading role in a three-act performance.

"I know you were expecting Annabelle, but. . ." Pricilla worked to keep her emotions suppressed despite the knot of fear welling up inside her chest. She could do this. "But I'm here instead."

"Great." He popped the tab of his drink and took a swig. "A nosy old woman trying to play the role of Nancy Drew."

"Ouch. You know you were much more pleasant in your role of respectable college student." Pricilla forced herself to look him in the eye and hold her ground. "So, I guess we both know why you're here?"

He shrugged, and she couldn't help but wonder if he really felt as calm as he looked. The whole ensemble—T-shirt, Windbreaker, jogging shorts, and white tennis shoes—gave him the generic look of any other morning jogger. "Is this some nutty idea of Mrs. Pierce's to pay me to be quiet?"

"Because half of the diamonds were your father's?"

His face paled. "How did you—"

"What if I told you there were no diamonds hidden beneath the bookshelf?"

"What?"

Pricilla watched his reaction. "You didn't get a chance to find out, did you, so you're not sure what was in there?"

"Stop trying to play with my mind. I can't imagine Annabelle going to all this trouble for a handful of Monopoly money." He held up the ransom note they'd left. "This is proof enough that I was on the right track, and Annabelle was wise to believe I won't stop until I find it. It was supposed to be so simple."

"Simple, that is, until Reggie realized who you were? The son of his dead business partner."

"No." Darren shoved his hands into the front pockets of his navy blue Windbreaker. "So what now? You don't really expect me to leave without my father's fortune. I know it's mine. I found out about the existence of the diamonds from some notes of his I found last night. Unless you're in on this with the detective—"

Pricilla searched for the plausible response she'd memorized. "I would say that's highly unlikely, considering the detective has already arrested me once and had me hauled into the sheriff's office a second time because of this entire mess. The man doesn't exactly hold me in the highest regard."

He leaned against one of the cooler doors and combed his fingers through his hair. "This entire situation is ridiculous, you know. I suppose I led Mrs. Pierce to the diamonds last night when she caught me, though I didn't think she saw me. I should never have left without finding them."

"I am, or shall I say Annabelle is, prepared to make a deal with you. You want the diamonds. She wants you out of her life."

Darren smacked his fist against the door. "You know, I would have been halfway to Brazil with the diamonds by now if it hadn't been for a slight interruption in my plan. All I want is what is rightfully mine."

"Even if that means stooping to murder?"

"Reggie deserved to die. He killed my father." Darren grabbed Pricilla's arm. "You know, I'm tired of this. It's time we did this on my terms."

"And what are your terms, Darren?"

"Considering you've just become my hostage, that's none of your business."

20

Pricilla felt a sharp jab of pain shoot down her arm as Darren pulled her toward the front door of the store. Over a pot of tea the night before, she'd tried to plan what to do if Darren became aggressive, but Carter had assured her the police would be waiting in the wings to jump in at the first sign of trouble.

Well, she was sensing trouble.

Darren's grasp tightened. "You'd better not scream."

One look around the store revealed an empty spot at the counter. Where was that cashier? So much for Carter's assurances of coming to her rescue. Trying to pull away from Darren's grip, she knocked into a display of potato chips. The cans tumbled off the shelf and onto the floor. She lost her footing for an instant as she tripped over one of them, but his hold on her arm never loosened.

She had no one to blame but herself. They'd been looking for more than a simple burglary conviction. She'd wanted a murder confession that would clear Annabelle's name and had believed that raising the stakes would increase the chances Darren would confess. It had taken her an hour and three pieces of her peanut butter pie to convince Carter that out of all the people Darren knew, she was the one he would talk to.

That cockamamie assessment of hers had proven correct. Darren had confessed to her and straight into the hidden microphone of the detective's state-of-the-art recording technology that had picked up every syllable of the man's confession. Its technological advances better not fall short when it came to the ability to rescue hostages and announce their distress.

As Darren's grip tightened, Max's face appeared unexpectedly in the recesses of her mind. In facing the wrath of a murderer, she suddenly realized what a complete fool she'd been to send Max away. All her excuses to guard her heart no longer seemed important. She loved him. And now she might not get the chance to tell him again.

Pricilla tried to suck in some air. The room was starting to spin. She could make out the door ahead of her but still couldn't tell where the cashier was. She was out of breath and her arm was going to have a nasty bruise from Darren's tight hold. Something caught the corner of her eye as Darren pulled her around the last corner before they got to the automatic front door. Betting on her last chance, she grabbed a can of air freshener with her free hand and managed to pop the lid off with her thumb. Praying that her aim would be better than her common sense, she squeezed.

The effect was immediate. A howl rang out. The air smelled of fresh peaches and cinnamon before the room spun out of control. She felt a burst of pain at the back of her skull. Someone shouted.

Then everything went dark.

⌐

"Mom?"

Pricilla opened her eyes then shut them against

the glare of the sun. Her head pounded beneath the mental fog that enveloped her. "Nathan?"

"How do you feel?"

She forced her eyes open. Plastic seats, metal grill barrier, and the smell of peaches. . . This couldn't be happening. She was sitting in the parking lot of the convenience store in the back of a patrol car.

"Mom?"

"You asked how I feel? Like I have a hangover." She rubbed her temples with her fingertips and struggled to sit up then melted back into the seat. "Not that I've ever had one, but. . .what's going on?"

"You're in the back of Detective Carter's patrol car."

"I can see that, but why?"

Nathan scratched his head and rested against the open doorframe beside her. "You fainted."

"Fainted? I. . .I most certainly did not." Pricilla's eyes widened in horror. "That's impossible."

"As impossible as a person claiming they don't snore because they've never heard themselves. Trust me, you were out cold."

"I don't understand." The throbbing in her temples intensified. "What about Darren?"

Nathan nodded toward the front of the store where Darren leaned against the brick wall with a scowl on his face. "According to the detective, he's waiting for permission to leave so he can go down to the station to file a complaint against the department."

"What?" Pricilla shook her head and tried to clear the ringing noise. Obviously, movement was not a good idea. "I don't understand."

"I'm not sure I understand all of this either, considering I wasn't let in on the final details of this latest escapade of yours." Nathan squatted on the ground beside the car and took her hands. "We just dropped off Max at the airport, and he told me you were through with all of this, which was what I had gathered from yesterday's version of your plan. Then I got a call from Detective Carter a few minutes ago."

"The plan changed." Pricilla winced. So Max was gone, a fact that hurt worse than the growing headache. At least he hadn't seen her in all her humiliation. "We were going to trap Darren and get a confession."

"Well, that's the other interesting thing. The setup you were involved in didn't work. Instead of picking up your conversation with Darren, all that was recorded was John Denver playing in the background. The cashier, an undercover detective, sensed a problem and slapped the handcuffs on Darren, who now claims he was simply leading you outside for some fresh air because you were feeling faint."

She shook her head. This was too much information, too fast. And none of it what she wanted to hear. "And then I passed out?"

"Or hit your head. No one is completely sure what happened."

This was unbelievable. Aches from arthritis and occasional bouts with memory loss, yes, but fainting? "I've never fainted before in my life. Never."

Nathan laid a hand on her shoulder and squeezed gently. "You've been under a lot of pressure lately, Mom, between your job at the lodge, Reggie's murder, and your relationship with Max. I don't think that something like this should be totally unexpected."

"Fainting is what delicate women do in Victorian novels."

"No one would ever call you delicate, Mom."

"But my entire plan was for nothing."

Trisha arrived with a candy bar and a bottle of juice. "An ambulance is on its way, but I thought this might help if you have low blood sugar."

"I don't have low blood sugar—an ambulance?" Pricilla's fingers grasped the edge of the seat. She was not going anywhere in an ambulance.

"Take it. Please." Trisha held out the food. "The detective insisted on getting your head checked out just in case."

Pricilla frowned, ignoring the offer. "I doubt he was worried about a concussion when he said that."

"Mom, take the juice and candy bar."

She didn't feel like arguing, so she took the imposed gifts.

Trisha stood beside Nathan and wrapped her arm around his waist. "Did you hit your head?"

"I think so." Pricilla felt for sore spots with her hand then winced. "Of course, every muscle in my body is aching right now, so I'm not sure what happened."

A phone went off and Trish reached for her back pocket. "Hang on."

"Darren claims you slipped and hit your head on one of the shelves, Mom."

"Nonsense." The throbbing began to intensify. Maybe she had hit her head. She tried to remember exactly what happened. "We were talking, and somewhere in the midst of my questions he confessed to killing Reggie. That had been the plan, but then he must have panicked. He said he was taking me as his hostage."

Nathan frowned, and Pricilla looked away.

"I suppose fainting was a good move on your part, but Darren is still claiming to be the hero in this situation."

Pricilla jutted her chin up at Nathan's last words. "What did you say? The hero?"

"That's what the detective told me."

"This is ridiculous. Someone had to have seen something. What about the video surveillance in the store? All gas stations have security measures like that."

"You're finally awake, Mrs. Crumb?" Nathan moved aside as the detective stepped up to the car and knocked on the top of the roof with his knuckles. "How are you feeling?"

"Better until you had to make that awful noise."

"Sorry."

"I don't know what's going on, Detective, or what Darren told you, but he grabbed me." Pricilla pressed her hand against the door handle and pushed herself up out of the car as she addressed the detective. "He took me hostage—"

"Whoa, slow down, Mom." Nathan reached down to stop her ascent, but she stopped him with the flick of her hand.

"I'm fine."

"You still have to be checked out by a doctor—"

"He's right, Mrs. Crumb, but we've also run into a kink here. I assumed, like you've just said, that Darren tried to grab you, but he says otherwise. We've just been looking at the tape, and unfortunately it isn't clear if Darren grabbed you or if you tripped and Darren was helping you. Low blood sugar perhaps—"

"I don't have low blood sugar." She threw the candy bar and drink into the patrol car. "I'm perfectly healthy."

"I thought I was, too, but somehow I managed to let you talk me into this ridiculous setup." The detective turned to Nathan. "My wife keeps nagging at me to show a little sympathy and listen to others, so I thought, why not? Some of Mrs. Crumb's instincts have in the past proven to be valid, so why not go out on a limb and figure out a way to catch this guy once and for all. Look where Solomon's wisdom got me this time."

"Thanks for the vote of confidence." Pricilla leaned against the car. "But that doesn't change the fact that I still don't understand what happened."

Carter shoved his glasses up the bridge of his nose. "Not only did we not get any sort of confession from Darren—"

"Nathan told me. That wasn't my fault—"

"He also said that he's planning to sue the department." Carter held out his hand. "I'd like my microphone back, please. At least I won't get written up for losing department property along with all my other blunders today."

"It doesn't work." Pricilla worked to unfasten the microphone from inside her blouse pocket.

"Did you have to remind me?"

"Sorry." The hook snagged then finally came loose. "He did confess, you know."

"So you say, but at the moment I can't do anything about it. I'd say that sums up the situation quite nicely."

She held up the faulty device, then with a flare of dramatics dropped it into his open hand. "What about the spray can? Doesn't that prove I was trying to defend myself?"

"You managed to miss Darren and instead hit Detective Markham, who was working the counter. He's in the bathroom, flushing out his eyes. Who's to say who you were aiming at?"

"A bout of insanity, I suppose you'd like to think?"

"A defense lawyer *would* claim something like that."

She ignored his comment. "Does Annabelle get the diamonds?"

"I'm sure that will involve piles of legal hassles. With no physical evidence that he was planning to steal the diamonds, it's going to take a top prosecutor to stop him from claiming a share, which in reality might actually be his."

"I'll testify."

"Don't even go there for now. You're officially off the case. Besides, what we have now is his word against yours. It's a mess. A complete mess." The detective dropped the microphone into his pocket and frowned. "The ambulance just pulled in, finally. I want you completely checked out. I don't need two complaints against the department in one day. I'm never going to hear the end of this as it is."

Trisha rushed to the car, her hands behind her back and a serious expression on her face. "Pricilla, I. . .that was Dad on the phone. He called from the airport to see if he forgot his shaving kit at my house. He said he didn't know about the plan, and—"

"You told him?"

Trisha nodded slowly. "He's meeting us at the hospital."

Pricilla's heart lurched. She'd managed to completely botch her chance at catching Reggie's murderer, but maybe there was a chance to save her relationship with the man she loved.

⸺

Max punched the elevator button and frowned at the closed doors. How long did it take for a box the size of a refrigerator carton to drop one story, open its doors, and suck him in? He hated elevators. He hated hospitals even more. Hated the smells, and the green walls, and the constant beeps and whirring sounds of machines. It brought back too many memories of doctor's appointments, hospital stays. . .and Violet.

Violet.

Sometimes it seemed as if she'd been gone forever. Other days it seemed like only yesterday. He'd buried those feelings so deep, he hadn't allowed himself to remember the pain anymore. Pricilla had, though, and he'd ended up losing her because she still felt the heartache of losing someone she loved.

He punched the button again. "I blew it, Lord."

Not that he would have given up forty years of marriage because the ending hurt. Never. But he should have been more patient with Pricilla. Instead of leaving, he should have recognized her fear and waited for her. Things might have turned out differently.

Where are the stairs?

He took a step back and stared down the hallway.

"Dad?"

"Trish."

His daughter strode toward him and smiled. "What are you doing?"

"They told me they put Pricilla in a room upstairs."

"I'll take you to her." She motioned with her hand. "She's down the hallway in the emergency room."

"They told me—"

"Someone told you wrong, Dad. And by the way, she's going to be fine. You can stop worrying." She wrapped her hand around his arm and started walking. "Being here brings back memories of Mom, doesn't it?"

"Your mom hated the hospital, but she never showed it. Always had a smile for the nurses and a good joke for the doctors. I could never be that way. I'd moan and complain until they kicked me out on my backside."

Trish's laugh faded as he passed a bulletin board. Pleas for blood donors. . . cancer support groups. . . information on Alzheimer's. . .

There was too much pain in the world.

Max squeezed his daughter's arm. "Have you ever thought about why?"

"Why what?"

"Why there is so much pain in this world." Their footsteps echoed down the empty hallway. "I lost your mother. Pricilla lost Marty. Annabelle losing Reggie has brought nothing but heartache to her family, and even to Pricilla, who managed to get herself involved in the entire mess."

"That's Pricilla, Dad. Saying she cares is never enough. She has to jump in and fix everything."

"That's what I love about her. Loved."

She nudged him with her elbow. "You were right the first time, Dad. You love her and she loves you. Why don't you just swallow your pride and give Pricilla the time she needs. She let you go because you weren't ready to wait for her."

"Time I should have been willing to give her."

Max frowned, frustrated at his own stubbornness. He hadn't been willing to wait for the best thing he had going for him in his life. And it had taken almost losing Pricilla to realize she was worth waiting for. For as long as it took. They might not have forty years ahead of them, but he'd take whatever he could get. Because it would be spent with Pricilla. Now he just had to pray that God would give them another chance.

Trish laced her fingers through his and squeezed. "You used to tell me that when God created the world, though, everything He made was good. Sin is what separated us from God. Never God Himself. From the very beginning He's been trying to draw men back to Him. Jesus was the ultimate sacrifice to bring us back to Him."

"Did I ever tell you what a wise daughter I have?

I think I just needed to be reminded of what was true." Max stopped at the door to the emergency room and turned to Trisha. "And because I suppose at times it's easier to blame the Creator instead of man's decisions."

"Pain is a part of life, but don't ever let it stop you from living." Trisha reached up and planted a kiss on his cheek. "Now, get in there and talk to her."

Max took a deep breath and crossed the emergency room floor until he got to room 3. He tapped on the door and heard her say "Come in."

Something in his heart trembled when he saw her. Oh, yes. He loved her. Still. "Hi."

Pricilla reached up and tried to fix her disheveled hair.

He sat down beside her on the narrow bed. "Don't worry about it. You'll always look beautiful to me. Though I didn't realize that your plan to save Annabelle involved your taking down a murderer and almost getting yourself killed."

"Killed? Obviously reports of my death have been highly exaggerated." She fiddled with the edge of the bed sheet. "The whole plan was a disaster. If you think the detective didn't like me before. . .well, let's just say I'm sure if it were up to him he'd have me thrown back into one of his jail cells."

He decided to ignore her last comment. Even Carter couldn't do that. "What did the doctor say?"

She touched the side of her head with her hand. "A mild concussion. Nothing to worry about."

From the moment he'd entered the room, he'd

tried to gauge her reaction to his presence, and so far he didn't think he was doing very well. She'd yet to smile at him or give any clue that she even wanted him in the room. Perhaps she was simply still frazzled from her experience at the convenience store.

Don't let pain stop you from living.

Trish had been right. He was ready to live again. And Pricilla had brought life back to him. She might kick him out and tell him she never wanted to see him again, but she was going to hear him out.

"Max, I've been a complete fool—"

"Pricilla, I need to say something to you—"

They spoke at the same time.

She held up her hand and shook her head. "Me first. Please. Something happened to me inside that convenience store. When I found out that Darren was the man who had killed Reggie, I knew he wouldn't think twice about murdering me as well. But what scared me the most was the fact that I'd lose you. I should have never let you walk away, Max." She reached out and grasped his hand. "I love you."

Max trembled at her touch. She really loved him? "So I haven't lost you?"

She shook her head and squeezed his hand. "What were you going to say?"

"I. . .I was ready to board the plane this morning and walk out of your life." He caught her gaze. "When Trish told me what had happened, I knew I'd made the biggest mistake of my life. I shouldn't have left. I gave up too soon on us, and I'm not ready to throw away the chance we have for love. Neither of us knows what the future holds. I could die from a heart attack tomorrow, but being together today would make it worth it. Or we could both live another thirty years until we're half senile, and have lost all our teeth, or at least can't remember where we've put them—"

"Oh, Max."

Pricilla's smile made his pulse race

"Let's promise not to worry about what might happen tomorrow." He reached up to wipe away the tear that slid across her cheek then kissed her gently on the lips. "Pricilla, I want you to be my wife. Will you marry me?"

21

Two days later Pricilla glanced at Max like a smitten schoolgirl while Misty worked her way around the table, serving individual dessert plates of passion fruit tarts. The room was filled with the sweet scent of the buttery crust with its fruit filling and piped meringue on top, but all Pricilla's senses could take in at the moment was Max. Blue eyes stared back at her, leaving her feeling tipsy despite the fact that not a drop of alcohol had been served during tonight's feast.

"The dinner is spectacular, but even more so is the hostess." Max reached for her hand then brought it to his lips like the romantic hero straight out of a black and white movie.

Pricilla felt a blush creep up her cheeks as she took a bite of the dessert and savored the tropical taste of the passion fruit. As she'd planned, the atmosphere was perfect. A centerpiece of fresh-cut flowers from the garden and an arrangement of lit candles offered a warm glow to the room, adding yellow radiance to the dimmed lighting. A fire crackled in the fireplace, more for ambiance than for the need of warmth on the drizzly spring night. Even the mahogany table had been set for eight with the lodge's finest gold-rimmed white china, crystal glasses, and sterling silverware.

The setting was perfect. Everything was perfect. Pricilla Crumb was sixty-five years old and hosting her own engagement party. . .to Max. Life didn't get much better than this.

Trish and Nathan had joined them for the celebration along with Annabelle, her children, and new son-in-law. The only downside of the evening was the fact that Darren hadn't been arrested in connection to Reggie's death, and they still didn't know what the outcome would be regarding the investigation. The detective had promised, though, that he would do everything he could to put a close to the case as soon as possible. At least the spotlight had been taken off Annabelle for the moment.

Pricilla's instincts might not have been far off, but the whole experience with her jaunt as a detective—amateurish as it might have been—had taught her a number of important lessons. She had learned the importance of waiting on God instead of jumping into things on her own. It was time to allow God to curb her impulsivities and let Him be the Lord of her life. Additionally, the conflict at the convenience store had taught her that life was short and unpredictable. One never knew what was around the next corner. . .a corner she now knew she wanted to take with Max.

Stewart, who sat across from her, set his fork on his plate and cleared his throat. "Mrs. Crumb, I. . .well. . . I just wanted to apologize. My behavior over the past few weeks has been anything but appropriate. Through my father's death, I was forced to see what happens when revenge and anger take hold of a person. It made me realize that I want to be on the right side of the law. I'm going back to school in the fall and am going to finish my degree in forensic science. Who knows, maybe one day Detective Carter will hire me."

"That's wonderful, Stewart." Pricilla turned to the young man's mother. "Annabelle, you must be so proud of his resolution."

"Very proud." The spark that had been missing for weeks was finally back in Annabelle's eyes.

"You're not the only one with plans to go back to school, little brother." Ezri's broad smile lit up the room. "Kent and I are going to finish our last year of school then return to Rendezvous to help Mom run the business. Kent will have a degree in business, and we want to not only expand the mail-order side of the bakery, but add an ice cream parlor."

"We can certainly use another booming business in this town." Nathan nodded his approval.

"Your mother was the one who brought us all together." Ezri smoothed the wide collar of her shirt and held up her glass of cider. "Thank you, Mrs. Crumb."

Pricilla's eyes moistened with tears. "You're welcome, Ezri."

"Since we're all confessing. . ." Annabelle cleared her throat. "I know a lot can happen in the next year or two, but just the thought of having my kids living nearby brings me a peace. And best of all, I've rededicated my life to Christ. It's time I went forward and became the example and leader I need to be to my children."

The doorbell rang, interrupting the rounds of well wishes for the Pierce family. "Who could that be?"

A moment later Misty announced Detective Carter.

Pricilla pushed her chair back and stood. "Why, Detective Carter. We weren't expecting you."

Carter took off his raincoat and handed it to Misty.

"What's the occasion? I seem to have crashed a party."

Pricilla felt a blush creep up her cheeks. "It's an engagement party. . .for Max and me."

Carter ran his hand across his balding head and smiled. "It looks as if congratulations are in order."

"We've just finished dinner, but if you'd like some dessert—"

"No, please, sit down. What I have to say won't take long." He rested his hand against the end chair where Nathan was sitting. "In fact, this setting couldn't be more perfect. I've always wanted to hold a dinner party during which I reveal the real murderer among the assembled list of suspects."

Several let out audible gasps at the detective's announcement. Color drained from Annabelle's face. Pricilla's stomach knotted into a ball. She wasn't going to allow him to ruin this party no matter what the news.

"Detective Carter, please. We are celebrating tonight."

"I suppose then that you don't want to hear that I made an arrest today and am in the process of closing the case."

"You're what?" Pricilla sat back down in her chair.

"You heard me right. I'm closing the case." The detective took off his glasses and cleaned them with the bottom of his shirt. "You might not believe this, but while our setup at the convenience store might not have worked, I managed to get a full confession out of Darren."

Pricilla's brow narrowed in impatience, but she

realized that the detective was enjoying his theatrics.

The detective put his glasses back on. "I've spent the past forty-eight hours gathering evidence, and from what I have so far, Darren had always been convinced that Reggie killed his father. A fact, I suppose, that we might never be able to prove. Needless to say, Darren believed it. His plan was to take revenge on his father's death and get his hands on the diamonds. He spent the last month methodically searching the house for the diamonds."

Annabelle shook her head. "Explaining why things were always out of place. And why I thought I'd lost one of my house keys."

"Add to that, he figured that your family would have plenty of motivation to kill Reggie if he played you all against each other. He was the one who typed up the phony *unsigned* will to throw me off the trail."

Annabelle fingered her glass and stared at the clear liquid. "So while my husband didn't live the life of a saint, at least he didn't turn on his family in his last moments."

"You can be assured of that, Mrs. Pierce."

Pricilla had had enough of the detective's theatrics. "I still don't understand how you got him to confess. Last I heard he was planning to sue the department."

Carter smiled. "Let's say that microphone ended up working after all."

Pricilla leaned forward. "You actually taped his confession?"

"Not exactly. He saw you give me back the microphone with your typical dramatic flair, and he thought he'd been busted. I was able to play on that belief and while he thought he was striking a deal with me for a lesser sentence, yesterday he managed to turn himself over for a certain conviction."

Max laughed. "That's unbelievable."

Annabelle rested her arm on her daughter's shoulder. "So does that mean that my family and I are innocent now in the law's eyes?"

"Yes, it does." Carter tapped his fingers against the chair then took a step backward. "I have to run, but I thought you would all enjoy hearing the news."

Nathan held up his glass as the detective grabbed his coat and left the room. "I'd like to propose a toast. To closure for Annabelle and her family, and to the future of Max and Pricilla."

"Here, here!"

Trish winked at her father. "Have you two set a date for the wedding?"

Pricilla looked at Max and offered a wry grin. "Not yet."

"We have." Nathan squeezed Trisha's hand. "October 17."

Pricilla sighed. "I'd say we have some work ahead of us, Max. Wedding dates, decorations—"

"That settles it, sweetheart." Max reached out and took Pricilla's hand. "We're eloping—"

"And deprive me of seeing my mother marry?" Nathan's brow rose. "I think I remember a certain person balking at the idea of her only son eloping."

"It looks as if setting a date is inevitable." Max groaned but didn't lose the twinkle in his eye as he turned to Pricilla. "Something I'm not complaining about one bit."

Pricilla beamed at Max's smile and the lighthearted banter that filled the room, thanking God for once again bringing a second chance at happiness into her life.

Currently, Lisa and her husband, along with their three children, are working in Mozambique as church planters. Lisa speaks French and is learning Portuguese. Life is busy between ministry and home school, but she loves her time to escape into another world and write and sees this work as an extension of her ministry.

Besides writing, Lisa loves to travel. She and her husband have visited over twenty countries throughout Europe and Africa. She's also spent time in Japan and Brazil. One of her favorite pastimes is learning to cook exotic dishes from around the world.

You may correspond with this author by writing:
Lisa Harris
Author Relations
PO Box 721
Uhrichsville, OH 44683

A Letter to Our Readers

Dear Reader:

In order to help us satisfy your quest for more great mystery stories, we would appreciate it if you would take a few minutes to respond to the following questions. We welcome your comments and read each form and letter we receive. When completed, please return to:

Fiction Editor
Heartsong Presents—MYSTERIES!
PO Box 721
Uhrichsville, Ohio 44683

Did you enjoy reading *Baker's Fatal Dozen* by Lisa Harris?

Very much! I would like to see more books like this!
The one thing I particularly enjoyed about this story was:

_____

_____

_____

Moderately. I would have enjoyed it more if:

_____

_____

_____

Are you a member of the HP—MYSTERIES! Book Club?
◯ Yes ◯ No

If no, where did you purchase this book?

_____

Please rate the following elements using a scale of 1 (poor) to 10 (superior):

___ Main character/sleuth   ___ Romance elements

___ Inspirational theme   ___ Secondary characters

___ Setting   ___ Mystery plot

How would you rate the cover design on a scale of 1 (poor) to 5 (superior)? _____

What themes/settings would you like to see in future **Heartsong Presents—MYSTERIES!** selections? ———

_____

_____

_____

Please check your age range:
- Q Under 18   Q 18–24
- Q 25–34   Q 35–45
- Q 46–55   Q Over 55

Name: _____

Occupation: _____

Address: _____

E-mail address: _____

HEARTSONG
PRESENTS
MYSTERIES

Think you can outwit clever sleuths or unravel twisted plots?
If so, it's time to match your mystery-solving skills
against the lovable sleuths of
Heartsong Presents—MYSTERIES!

You know the feeling—you're so engrossed in a book that you can't put it down, even if the clock is chiming midnight. You love trying to solve the mystery right along with the amateur sleuth who's in the midst of some serious detective work.

Now escape with brand-new cozy mysteries from *Heartsong Presents—MYSTERIES!* Each one is guaranteed to challenge your mind, warm your heart, touch your spirit—and put your sleuthing skills to the ultimate test. These are charming mysteries, filled with tantalizing plots and multifaceted (and often quirky) characters, but with satisfying endings that make sense.

Each cozy mystery is approximately 250 pages long, engaging your puzzle-solving abilities from the opening pages. Reading these new lighthearted, inspirational mysteries, you'll find out "whodunit" without all the gore and violence. And you'll love the romantic thread that runs through each book, too!

**Look forward to receiving mysteries like this on a regular basis—
join today and receive 4 FREE books with your
first 4 book club selections!**

As a member of the *Heartsong Presents—MYSTERIES! Book Club*, four of the newest releases in cozy, contemporary, full-length mysteries will be delivered to your door every six weeks for the low price of $13.99. *And shipping and handling is FREE!*

YES! Sign me up for **Heartsong Presents—MYSTERIES!**

NEW MEMBERSHIPS WILL BE SHIPPED IMMEDIATELY!
Send no money now. We'll bill you only $13.99 postpaid with your first shipment of four books. Or for faster action, call 1-740-922-7280.

NAME _____

ADDRESS_____

CITY_____ ST_____ ZIP_____

**Mail to: HEARTSONG MYSTERIES,
PO Box 721, Uhrichsville, Ohio 44683
Or sign up at WWW.HEARTSONGMYSTERIES.COM**